Attracted to a woman he shouldn't be, all because of the color of her skin, Sheriff Christopher Weatherby is conflicted, unsure of what to do with the passion that is building inside him. It is his job to help Lillian Pearl Porter solve her parents murder, but as the truth starts unraveling, it seems secrets are around every corner, all involving the woman he finds himself drawn to.

When Lilly returns to her parents' hometown after their deaths, she is met with the racism, discrimination and secrets that surround the small town of Kittrell, North Carolina. Determination flows through Lilly as she ventures on, fighting against the walls of segregation. She finds herself falling for a man who is forbidden. A love so strong that it pushes against the laws.

Will Lilly and Christopher be able to control their love or will their attraction end, just like Lilly's parents — in death?

Skin Deep
Copyright © 2020 Gen Ryan
ISBN: 978-1-4874-2769-6
Cover art by Martine Jardin

Published by eXtasy Books Inc or
Devine Destinies, an imprint of eXtasy Books Inc

Look for us online at:
www.eXtasybooks.com or www.devinedestinies.com

SKIN DEEP

BY

GEN RYAN

DEDICATION

To my daughter, Emma Marie, who has taught me so much about love. To my unborn son, Grayson Ty, may you never question how much you are loved.

CHAPTER ONE: IRIS

1937

"**Y**ou *think just because you shacked up with a white man, I won't whip your ass?*"

I glanced up. His grin spread across his face as though he'd won the lottery. I suppose I was his winnings. Me, Iris Porter. The woman who loved the wealthiest man in Kittrell, North Carolina. Normally no one would bat an eye, but I'm black and I used to be a servant in the house of the father of my partner, Charles.

My skin isn't too dark, like coffee when you add a little cream, so I'd been lucky to be a house servant. I hadn't made a lot of money, but I had been treated decently. Charles and I fell in love the moment I stepped foot in his house. We didn't see differences—skin color, social class, or anything else. There was just us and we were in love.

But that was decades ago. That time had been even more challenging than it was now. More hate, more violence.

As I clung onto the tree, parts of my body exposed, the hate and fear I'd experienced all those years ago resurfaced. I'd never experienced violence, but my mother had told stories of her father, her brothers, all suffering physical and emotional torment through times that I was thankful not to have witnessed. The stories were enough to bring me to tears and to question how humanity could be so cruel. I had thought times were different now. The violence not as rampant, whipping a thing of the past. It was meant to be, but now, as I was being

1

lashed, I imagined how my ancestors felt — my father who I had never got to know, taken from this world too soon, all because of the color of his skin.

The whip struck me, and a trickle of blood wept down my back. The pain was unbearable, and I forced myself not to cry with each strike. I bit my lips so hard they cracked and bled under the pressure, but I didn't make a sound. I didn't want to give him the satisfaction.

"Please stop this. We're leaving. We won't come back. I just wanted to bury my father." I turned my head and saw Charles, my soulmate, the man I was forbidden to love. Tears streamed down his face. He was tied, there we no marks marring his skin, but I knew his torture was watching me as each strike hit my body. I gave him a strained smile as a tear escaped my eyes.

The years had been kind to us. Those years had blessed us with a daughter, Lillian Pearl Porter. She was twenty-three, beautiful, kind, and determined. I was proud of those traits, but also scared. Scared of her determination and how she would react when she found out what had happened to her father and me. She wouldn't let it go, and I feared more for her than I did for the pain I knew I had yet to endure.

"You made the mistake of coming back here. Flaunting your sinful relationship." He laughed. "At least you didn't bring that daughter of yours, Lilly."

I fought against the chains that bound me, and Charles wrestled with his at the sound of our daughter's name. The man who held us captive had hit a nerve, and by the sly smile that formed on his face, he knew it too.

"Ahh." He swung the whip in his hand. "Lilly is her name isn't it?" He moved closer to me, his breath sour from all the alcohol he'd drunk. "If she's half as beautiful as you, I can't wait to get a taste." He lashed my open wounds with the leather, each strike more painful than the last. I still didn't make any noise, though, even at the mention of Lilly. I had learned from my mother, and that lesson had forever stuck with me.

Don't make a sound. Never let them know your pain.

"You think you're tough?"

Another crack of the whip sent me further into my mind. I thought of Lilly, when she was younger. Her pudgy face, her carefree childhood. She had grown up in a place where she'd been loved and respected regardless of the color of her skin. Things weren't perfect. We had dealt with racism, but it wasn't as bad as it was in the South.

More cracks of the whip eventually sent my body into a numb state. I was thankful when that came because I didn't have to hide. I didn't have to pretend.

"Please just let her go." Charles fought against his chains, the rattling bringing me out of my daydream. "Why are you doing this?"

"Because. This shouldn't be. You two shouldn't be. It's a disgrace, and your damn father should have taught you a lesson when he had the chance."

"My father didn't agree with my choices when it came to Iris, but he let me go. Because although we disagreed, violence, lynching, killing, it was never an option," Charles replied. "So, let her go! Take it out on me. Whip me."

He smiled, and the breeze returned and bent the trees. They swayed sympathetically, creaking under the pressure of the wind. They were like my body, molding, threatening to break at any moment with each crack of that whip.

"Charles, It's okay honey. It's going to be okay." Our eyes met. The kindness, the love I had seen the first day I laid eyes on him, still there, just more of it. More profound, more sincere.

"Don't leave me, Iris, not yet," Charles whispered.

I wanted to stay with Charles. Nothing would have made me happier than to live out the rest of our days together. We

3

were playing with borrowed time. Time that we had snuck away and stole. I wish I could say our love story had been perfect, but our love was built on heartache and broken laws.

My mind held on to a memory as the pain ravaged my already broken body.

"Come away with me." Charles kissed my temple and held my hand in his. What I felt every time he was with me was unlike anything else. It was like a warm blanket on a cool day. Charles brought me security and comfort. He gave me love.

We were down by the lake where we often snuck away to be together. He was on break from college, and I relished the time I had when he was back.

"What about your father?" I gave him a questioning glance. "And my mom. I can't leave her." I took my hand out of his. "What about Fredrick. Your best friend?"

I fought back the emotions that battered me. Excitement. Hope. Fear. I wanted to go away with him. So badly that it hurt. But I didn't want him to regret his life. Things would be much simpler if he chose someone else to spend his life with. Someone where he could stay in North Carolina and inherit his family's estate and money. Because loving me meant he'd have to give up those things.

"Stop," Charles said with a laugh.

"Stop what?" I put my arms across my chest.

"Over thinking everything." He kissed my forehead. "What if I told you I already talked with your mother?"

My heart rate quickened as I looked around making sure no one could hear his words. "No," I said shaking my head.

"Yes," he whispered against my hair. "Plus, Fredrick, he's changed. He's too busy getting in with the wrong crowd. He's so invested in trying to fit in somewhere that I'm not sure who he is anymore."

I nodded. We had all been friends once. Until Fredrick had tried to kiss me and I slapped him. I didn't tell him about Charles and me, but he didn't take kindly to my rejection. Things had been strained between us all ever since. Charles and I fought to keep our light, but something about Fredrick changed, and suddenly Charles and I meant nothing to him.

"And your mother. Well, she gave me her blessing if I finished this last semester at law school. She said over her dead body would she let me take you away without a good profession to take care of you."

The world was spinning. I loved Charles. He was it for me and always would be, but it was hard for us to be together. Especially here in North Carolina. We'd always have to hide our love. The places where we could be together more openly were far away from here. Far away from the hate, the pain, the years my family had spent being servants. I could be free to love the man who saw me as a woman. No color. Just someone worthy of being loved.

"How? When?" I jumped up.

Charles laughed again, pulling me down into his lap. "Is that a yes?" he asked, raising his eyebrow.

I grinned. "Yes!"

He stood, pulling me with him. He twirled me around, and this time his kiss was planted firmly on my lips. My breath hitched in my throat, my body taking on a mind of its own as Charles kissed me.

"Philadelphia, Iris. Me and you. I'll start my own practice, and we can be happy and have tons of babies."

I let out a contented sigh against his chest.

"Nothing can get in our way," Charles said while he rubbed my back.

I looked up at the man I loved, hoping his words were true and nothing would get in our way. I buried the sinking feeling deep in my chest and enjoyed the moment with him because our future was bright. We didn't care about normalcy or what society declared. We loved each other, and love was enough for us to risk it all.

I smiled, the tears I had allowed to escape making their way into my mouth. The whipping continued, my focus shifting back to Lilly, to Charles, and finally, never returning from the memories that I escaped into. It was peaceful. There was no more pain. No more heartache, and for that I was thankful. Before I heard no more, there was a gun shot, once, then twice. Then Charles was there, reaching his hand to me. I took it and together, in silence, we slipped away.

I left everything that had happened in the woods, left my earthly body chained to that tree where I had been whipped to death. Charles and I might have been free from pain, but Lillian, she'd find that tree, she'd find that pain, and I almost felt sorry for that man—the one who had tortured us, killed us. All because we had loved fiercely, so deeply that we had seen no race. I knew she'd make him pay.

Chapter Two: Christopher

1937

I stepped out into the heat of the afternoon sun. It was only eight a.m., and I was already sweating. There was nothing quite like July in North Carolina.

I followed the sounds of the voices that were set back in the woods. I was used to attending the consequences of all sorts of brainless activities carried out by locals with little better to do with their time. This call, however, wasn't idiotic. This was murder.

I'd never been called to a murder case before. There was no violent crime other than a few drunken brawls in my hometown. There might have been some accidental deaths due to stupidity or too much drink, but this case — apparently there was no denying foul play.

"Sheriff." Branson, one of my deputies, was as white as a ghost. "This is the stuff of nightmares." He gulped.

"What do we have?" I headed to the tree, then stumbled back. I didn't care what training I'd had — nothing prepared a person for the brutality that was in front of me.

"Jesus Christ," I mumbled.

Branson was long gone and heaving his breakfast nearby. A woman was tied to the tree. She wore a beautiful white dress that was now stained with her blood. Gashes were torn through the fabric of her dress, deep wounds covering her back. I tried to glance at anything other than the body in front of me. Branson was back by my side and having trouble staying focused, but I couldn't blame him. We'd been told about things like this, we'd just never encountered them. I brushed her hair away that was hanging and matted in front of her eyes. She had stunning features, skin like mocha.

That was what had gotten her into this situation, the color of her skin, the person that she'd loved. I shook my head at the craziness of my thoughts. No one should be murdered, but being murdered because of who you loved? I'd never understood it. Hate was a powerful thing, and it made people do crazy things. No one deserved this torture and abuse.

I made notes as I inspected around the body. I saw a boot print, a little smaller than my size twelve, but there wasn't anything else of value. I moved on to Charles. His death seemed less gruesome. Although he looked as though he'd experienced less torture than Iris, I knew he'd no doubt suffered watching and listening to his wife's beating. Other than the single gunshot wound to the head, and one on his leg, there was no blood covering his body nor wounds on his back. However, Charles was leaned closer to Iris, and his hand was open towards her.

Even in death, he longs to be near her.

"Sheriff, I have the guy who found the bodies sitting in the car." Branson gagged then refocused. "Whenever you want to question him."

I patted him on the shoulder. "Thanks. The medical examiner just showed up to take away the bodies. I want to talk to him. Can you interview the witness for me?"

Branson's face regained some color. Branson was equipped to handle the M.E. but he was struggling. Hell, I was struggling, but I hadn't thrown up, yet.

"Yes, sir. No problem." He nodded.

"Sheriff." Dr. Hicks, the M.E., bent over Iris and started poking at her body. Unlike Branson and I, Dr. Hicks appeared unfazed by what he saw.

Maybe he didn't care? Maybe like so many other people he

didn't see Iris as a person. Didn't see her as worthy of an investigation. Damn. I'd have to contend with judgement because of who she was and what she and Charles stood for. Equality. Love.

"What caused her death, Doc? Any ideas?" I had my pen ready to go. I needed something, a break that I could take back to my father to express how important this case was.

It was going to be difficult to convince him to pool our scarce resources, both financially and for manpower. Normally, I wouldn't try to persuade my father to do anything. I'd brush things aside as he wanted. Standing here, looking at Iris' body and how Charles was reaching out for his wife one last time, even as his life was being threatened, it didn't matter to me what color their skin was. They deserved justice.

"Woman probably died of her wounds. I don't see any other issues at first glance." He chuckled. "This guy" —he made a fake gun with his hand—"boom. Gunshot wound to the head. And one sympathizer dead."

I'd grown up around racism, but hearing a man who held such an educated position within our community joke and mock these people made my skin crawl and royally pissed me off. I fought back the urge to shove him up against the tree by his throat, make him eat my fist, and take back his words.

"Dr. Hicks, these people were murdered. Show them some respect, please." I tried to keep my voice calm and even-keeled but my annoyance seeped through in the tone.

"Son, don't tell me you're going soft?" He put his arm around me. "Ahhh." He let me go. "First time seeing this gruesome of a scene, huh?" He shook his head. "This" —he pointed to Iris' back—"is nothing compared to some of the beatings I saw when I was a boy." He shrugged. "They aren't people. Well I guess they are now, but they used to not be. Property is what they were, and we used to be able to do what we wanted with our property."

I stared at him in disbelief. Branson cleared his throat, and Dr. Hicks scurried away with mumbles of getting his equipment to transport the bodies. I didn't know what the fuck had just happened. I was beginning to realize that people I had known my entire life, respected, idolized in some respects, were bigoted in their beliefs, and it infuriated me.

How had I not realized it before?

"Sheriff, are you okay?" Branson looked at me curiously.

I nodded and listened to what Branson told me about his interview with the witness. All I heard was a whole lot of no leads and a desire to find the daughter to inform her that her parents had been murdered.

When I was done processing what I could of the crime scene, I drove away with a fire burning in my belly. A fire for justice and to do what was right. I knew it was going to be easier said than done, but I wouldn't back down, not even from my own father, the Mayor.

CHAPTER THREE: LILLY

1937

"Lillian!" Mr. Harrington, my boss, called out.

I inwardly groaned as I shuffled through the mounds of paperwork that were stacked in front of me. I stood, adjusting my stiff dress and smoothing back my hair. I walked past the multiple desks, filled with women all doing the same job that I did—a glorified secretary. Many of them didn't care what they were doing. It was an excuse to dress up, put on makeup, and flaunt around the office all day long with hopes of finding a husband. I wanted something more, to be something greater than what I was now. I had a degree in law. I could fight any one of these cases and win. But instead, I was forced to sit behind a desk looking through paperwork, smiling and batting my eyelashes when people came in. I hated it.

Mr. Harrington used my mind, though. Used my ideas and legal expertise whenever he could. I couldn't have the job title, or the credit, or anything that showed I was worthy of doing more than looking pretty.

"Yes, Mr. Harrington?" I poked my head into his office.

His round belly protruded through his overpriced suit jacket. "Please, have a seat." He stood, breathing heavily, then pulled out a chair for me. He wasn't a mean man, but he usually wasn't an overt gentleman.

I gulped loudly as I sat down, worried that I was about to be let go. I didn't need this job. My father, Charles, and mother, Iris, made sure that I never wanted for anything, but

11

this job was my only hope of someday becoming a lawyer. I didn't want to work for my dad. I wanted to do things on my own. Times were changing, and I intended to be at the forefront of those changes.

Mr. Harrington sat on the edge of the desk, which brought him much closer to me than I would have liked.

"What's going on, Mr. Harrington? You're acting, strange." I sat straighter in the chair as he sighed.

"I just received a phone call from a Sheriff Weatherby at the Kittrell police department." He leaned in, resting his hand quickly on my shoulder before tearing it away. "It's about your parents . . ."

My heart rate quickened, and suddenly the stiff dress became a noose around my body. I couldn't breathe, I couldn't think straight, as Mr. Harrington continued to explain what had happened.

My mother tied to a tree and whipped to death. I couldn't make sense of the words he was saying. My parents, the people who loved me, sheltered me from the hate that they had been forced to endure their entire lives, now victims of something they had run from all those years ago. It shouldn't be. It couldn't be. I'd never see their faces again. I'd never watch their love, their hope, despite many people telling them that their love was wrong.

"Lilly," Mr. Harrington rested his hand on my shoulder again, lingering a bit longer than before.

I knew it was meant to bring me comfort, but it didn't. I jumped.

"Are you okay? I'm sorry."

"Yes." I managed to croak out, pushing back the emotions that swirled within me. "Who did it? Who killed them?"

"Well, there are no suspects, so — "

Rage filled me and replaced the sadness as I gripped the ends of the chair, my nails digging into the fabric. No suspects, no investigation. Case closed.

"Meaning, my parents' killer will go free." I shook my head.

Mr. Harrington stood then started pacing the floor. "Lilly." His tone was condescending, and it further ignited my rage.

"Don't *Lilly* me. I respect you, Mr. Harrington, so I won't say to you what I really want to right now. The Kittrell Police department will not investigate their deaths because my mother was black," I said, matter-of-factly.

"That isn't the case. Apparently, there isn't enough evidence." He adjusted his shirt, seemingly trying to mask his discomfort at his blatant lie.

"Evidence!" I sprang up from the chair and stared at him. "The whip marks that I'm sure covered my mother's back aren't evidence enough?" Tears streamed down my face. I wanted to fall to the ground and curl into a ball. My parents were everything to me. The love they shared always made me believe that love conquered all. That it was freeing and worth everything.

But now? What did their love get them? I brushed away my tears before continuing. "And the gunshot wound to my father's head, while he was tied, wasn't self-inflicted. What more evidence do they need?" My voice was loud. Faces peered in the office window, and women gathered around.

"These things are tricky now."

I laughed, a fully-fledged belly laugh, at Mr. Harrington's audacity. Maybe in whatever world he lived — where he hired women, even black women, to look pretty and shuffle paperwork — times were changing. I still couldn't sit at the front of the bus. I still couldn't go to the same diners as some of the ladies from work because of the color of my skin.

Had I ever been hit? Subjected to the abuse that my mother had been subjected to in North Carolina? No. But times were not changing, and certainly not for the better. They were being disguised as something else. We were being thrown a bone in order to feel equal.

"A thing of the past? I have a stack of cases on my desk that are hate crimes. Do you not watch the news? Our nation is still divided. Hate is still rampant, and my parents died at its hands." I wouldn't back down. Not this time. I wouldn't be the good girl who sat behind my desk and smiled. I wouldn't let my parents die in vain. After all, hate had a face, we just didn't know who yet, but I intended to find out what had happened.

"I can only imagine what you're going through. Take a few days off for the funeral arrangements." Mr. Harrington sat in his chair—the weight of the situation written on his face. His frown accentuated the lines under his eyes, his age all too apparent.

I softened a little, letting my shoulders relax from the tension that had built up there. Delivering the news to me could not have been easy, but it didn't excuse his dismissal of what was in front of him. Two murders. I had always told my mother I'd make a difference in the world. No matter how small the solving of my parent's murder would be in the grand scheme of things, I had to start sometime and somewhere. That time was now.

"No," I replied, folding my hands calmly.

"No?"

"I'm going to need more than a few days. I'm going to Kittrell."

"For what, Lilly? You will get hurt. They aren't as accepting there as we are here," he warned.

"I know. That's what I'm counting on. That the bastard who murdered my parents will be stupid enough to try and stop me." I leaned over the desk. "Because I won't rest until he is behind bars and paying for what he did. Because I"—I choked back the tears—"I believe that regardless of the color of your skin, you can love who you want. Be with who you want. My parents believed in that. They had a love that was before their time and they died for that love. And I'm their daughter and I will die to prove that this hate must end. Now!"

Mr. Harrington couldn't argue with that. He sat there in silence, while I grabbed my belongings and tried my best to avoid the stares and whispers of the other women as I walked out of the office. I held my head high, but the tears streamed down my face. I vowed I would be my parents' voice, whatever the cost.

Chapter Four: Lilly

1937

"Afternoon, Lilly. You're home early!" Our neighbor, Mrs. Prescott, sat on her front porch and waved to me. She frowned when I turned to look at her.

I'm sure my face was stained with tears. They had dried, and each time I moved my face it was as if I were cracking. I didn't care, though. All I cared about was getting to my parents. Putting all my energy into getting answers.

"What's wrong, child? It looks like you've seen a ghost."

I moved to the fence that separated our properties then leaned on it. It didn't take away the weight of my parents' loss, but it was good to be resting against something after my walk home.

"I did see a ghost. My parents' ghosts," I whispered.

Mrs. Prescott was an old woman. She might have had one foot in the grave, but she made it her civic duty to know everything that was going on in our neighborhood, at all times. She still had a keen sense of hearing.

"What happened?" She slowly came down the porch steps.

I don't remember what else I said. I know I told her what had happened. My mind, though, went to another place. It hummed with all that I had to get done, giving me something to focus on other than the grief that clawed like a beast at my chest.

Grief took on a different face for everyone. Some held it close and cried in silence. Others shed tears whenever and

16

wherever they wanted. Me? I was in between. The tears fell, but I was silent, stuck in my own head and trying to make sense of a situation that could have been prevented if only our world were different. But that was wishful thinking and wishing wouldn't bring my parents back.

Mrs. Prescott took me into my home, guiding me with a concern that I appreciated. I wasn't fragile by any means, but it was nice to have someone look after me. I walked into the house that my parents and I had lived in since I was a baby. This time, everything around me buzzed with an unfamiliar energy. It was like the house knew of the loss I had suffered. Doors and floorboards creaked more than normal. Or maybe they always had, and I hadn't noticed before. The silence, though, was aching to be filled. The wind from an incoming storm shook the windows, and the sun that had been present that morning was gone. Everything had shifted, all energy now focused on loss and heartache.

I'd never see my mother's smiling face or hear my father's jokes, which he told from the morning paper, again. There were many memories in this house, and the thought of them swirled emotions inside me. My head started spinning and my vision blurred.

My parents are gone.

Part of me didn't know what I was going to do without them. Another part of me churned with hate for the person who had taken them away from me too soon.

I pushed those emotions aside. I had a lot to take care of if I intended to leave first thing tomorrow morning for North Carolina. Letting myself crumble and fall wasn't an option right now.

Mrs. Prescott and I contacted my father's clients and let them know that he would be unavailable indefinitely. That was the only explanation I gave. I didn't want to hear words of sympathy, or, worse, words of, "I told you so".

Once that was settled, Mrs. Prescott insisted on making me

some dinner. I headed to my room to pack. My room was bright, splashes of color on every surface. I loved being surrounded by vibrant colors.

The painted pictures taunted me with their swirls of yellows and greens, hints of hope and love. It was all a lie. A lie that I had forced myself to believe. I should have been angry more often. I should have felt with my parents, the pain of their youth, and I should have understood what they had been through. Because now I was stepping into territory that I had only ever heard stories about, only half-listening — saying that nothing like that would never happen to me. But here I was, living it. Running full steam ahead into the hate that my parents had tried to bury, the hate my parents had run away from.

I gathered my clothes and essentials for the trip. I'd never traveled alone, and while many, women especially, would be scared, I was determined. When I'd left my job this morning, I'd known what I had to do. Now, my mind and my body were in sync.

My mother and father had shielded me from a lot of things, but they made sure I wasn't weak. Anytime I asked a question, I received an honest and truthful response.

"Lilly." My mother brushed back my hair. "Lilly, my pretty girl."

A woman, with her two children, glared at us from the bench. She quickly put on their jackets and huffed as she dragged the kids behind her.

"They were my friends, Momma. Why's she taking them away?"

My mom's face crumbled at my question. I thought I'd done something wrong, that maybe I wasn't playing nice enough. I cried and cried, asking my mom if I was bad.

My mom let me cry, then sat me down on the bench next to her. "Lilly, do you know what racism is?"

I scrunched up my nose. Of course, I knew what it was. It was when my mommy and daddy had to go to certain restaurants to eat or when Mommy and I couldn't use certain water fountains.

I nodded. "That's why their mom took them away?" I picked at the flowers next to the bench. I didn't understand.

"It's because I'm black and your half-black. Some people don't like that. They think we don't deserve the same rights."

I tried to understand her words. They made me mad. "That's silly, mommy. We're all the same. Just different shades of beautiful."

She pulled me close to her chest. "My sweet child," she said, brushing back my hair again. "Remember that, because you will come across a lot of hate in this world."

I looked up at her tear stained face. "I'm going to change the world someday, Momma. I'm going to make it all go away."

She simply smiled at me and sent me off to play. I didn't want my mom to be sad anymore. I didn't understand adults. Why they had silly rules like where you could sit, or eat, or play based on color. I wanted to change it. Change the rules just to make sure I'd never have to see my mother cry again.

"Dinner's ready!" Mrs. Prescott yelled from downstairs.

I grabbed my bag and took one last glance at my room. I didn't know when I'd be back.

I joined Mrs. Prescott in the dining room for the last meal in my home. Tomorrow morning, I was heading to where it had all started, to where my parents had begun their love affair. The determination from earlier and from the memory was still there, a low rumble in my chest. But alongside that emotion was something swirling, nagging at me—fear. That was there too. I would use that fear. I would use it to propel me towards what I really longed for—change.

CHAPTER FIVE: CHRISTOPHER

1937

"I just think that this case warrants a closer look. That's all."
I switched the case file to my other arm, shoving it underneath my armpit.

As a sheriff in Kittrell, I was fiercely protective of it. It was my safe place, and even though it was small to most, it was my home.

"Drop it. It doesn't matter. There isn't enough evidence."

I gritted my teeth at my father's words. He was the Mayor of this town, Mayor Fredrick Weatherby. He had his hands in everything. He had the last say on what cases were worthy of my time, and well, Iris and Charles Porter weren't cutting it apparently. He hadn't been there—he hadn't been a part of what I had. Seeing Charles and Iris' dead bodies had affected me. I wanted to help them and for their story be told.

While I'd never been as bigoted as my father, I'd never fought for what I believed in or went against him. This case was different, and I knew the only way I could get those images out of my head was to investigate the murders.

"She was whipped to death. He was shot. It was murder. And that boot print . . ." I opened the folder and then flung the picture of Iris on his desk. "Look at her, dad. Don't you remember her?"

My father and Charles had been close friends before Charles moved away, leaving behind his entire life in order to be with the woman he loved. It was a story that the entire town talked about to this day. The scandal that baffled so many.

"I remember her." He barely glanced at the picture before he threw it across the table. "They're outsiders now. They don't get special treatment. They made their choice to fall in love and run off like the cowards that they were."

I handed him the picture again and caught the expression on his pale face as he flipped it over.

"Plus, that boot print is the size of pretty much every man in this town. It'll be like looking for a needle in a haystack."

"Special treatment? Investigating their deaths is my job. Not special treatment." I was getting angrier by the minute. I shouldn't have had to fight to take a case that clearly had murder written all over it.

"Well that costs money, and I handle the money in this town. So I say no!" My father never raised his voice. His tone was always low, always calm, but that raised voice was enough to make the hairs on my skin stand up on end.

As I stood before him, a grown man at twenty-six, he was still able to get under my skin. I shook off the timidity, wanting to remain focused on Iris and Charles, and not on the way my father was intimidating me with his shouting and overbearing nature.

"If the Philadelphia police get wind of this, they will be all over it. I don't want them here snooping around any more than you do." I was grasping here. The moment I had heard about these murders, I was a bit relieved. Relieved that I had something to do that would make a difference, put someone behind bars. That excitement had turned to disgust when I saw Iris and Charles' brutalized bodies. It had turned into retribution.

My father sighed. "I suppose you're right." He adjusted his tie and sat back, tipping his leather chair. "Shit, I don't want those nigger lovers out here sniffing around. They'll be all up our asses."

I cringed at the word. I'd never once used the word, but my father, my brother, hell, almost everyone I knew said it. We lived amongst black people, but things were separate here. They stayed on their side of town, we stayed on ours. I didn't have the same animosity toward them as many did. But I kept those thoughts to myself. For my own safety. I was slowly beginning to wonder what the cost of my own safety was worth. Was my well-being worth the life of Iris and Charles?

When did I begin to put my needs before doing what was right?

"Do a little investigating. Make it seem like you give a damn. As far as I'm concerned, their deaths were a long time coming."

I nodded. I had a lot more I wanted to stay, but I didn't want to push my luck.

A knock at the door ended our conversation abruptly. I was thankful for the interruption, because I couldn't listen to his damn bigotry anymore.

"Sheriff Weatherby? A woman just walked in downstairs asking for you. Something about those two murders." Scarlett, the secretary, grinned at my father, barely making eye contact as she addressed me.

My father hadn't been the most the loyal husband. My mother had died, probably never knowing how many children my father had had, or how many other women he had slept with. I was pretty sure he'd bedded half the women in town. And by the way Scarlett looked at him, he'd be adding her to his list, if he hadn't already.

"Thanks, Scarlett. I'll be right down." I glanced over at my father as he smiled at Scarlett "Seems I have my first lead."

He frowned. "Don't waste too much of your time on this," he mumbled, shuffling through his paperwork.

"Yes, Sir. Bare minimum at best," I said sarcastically.

He grunted, half-paying attention as he read something on his desk. "Good. Now go." He waved me off. "I have work to do. Someone has to keep this town running." He picked up his telephone and started barking orders at his secretary.

I sighed as I walked away, grateful that I wasn't on the receiving end of that phone call.

As I descended the stairs to go to the precinct, I saw her. The moment was like one of those picture films, where time stood still, and the woman's hair flowed in the breeze. Except this was in glorious technicolor, and her color was what bewildered me. Her skin was sun-kissed and much darker than my complexion. It reminded me of the caramel candies my mother would sneak to me when I was younger.

She turned her face. Her eyes, big and green, stood out against the perfection of her skin. I only took my focus away from her face when she adjusted herself, switching one leg that was crossed with the other. I followed her legs, their long shapely lines barely hidden under her form fitting, pale-pink dress. Before I could reach the bottom of the stairs, she stood, smoothed out her dress, then came toward me, extending her hand in a greeting.

"Hello. Sheriff Weatherby, I presume?"

I shook her hand, the force with which she squeezed and asserted herself making me grin. She wasn't like the docile women around here who would giggle and bat their eyes at me. She was different.

"Yes. How can I help you Miss . . ." I waited for a reply, taking a second to look closer at her. While her green eyes were exquisite against her skin, her face was heart-shaped, with full, plump lips, and cheeks that had a rosy tint to them. But it was her eyes, which barely moved when she smiled, that seemed to show her heartache and loss. I wanted to know what had occurred to her to take away her happiness.

"Call me Lillian." The edge of her lips curved slightly and gave way to two dimples. "Is there a place we can talk, Sheriff?" she asked, glancing around.

My interest was piqued. I wanted to know who she was, why she was here, but mostly, I wanted to keep her talking. Her voice had a command about it, yet a softness that demanded my attention. I couldn't help but want to listen to her.

"Sure. Right this way."

As we walked to my office, her high heels clacked against the floor. Heads turned to watch us. I was sure it was a sight. Lillian was beautiful, but it was her skin that turned those heads. She was clearly of mixed race. Something that we didn't get to see much around here.

"Please have a seat." I pulled out a chair for Lillian.

"I'd prefer to stand."

I scrunched my face at her rejection.

"Not trying to be rude, Sheriff. I just spent a day on a train." She yawned. "I've had my fair share of sitting." She stretched a bit, her dress tightening around her slender body. Everything about her made time stand still. Perfection was too tame a word to describe her presence. It wasn't only her physical attributes that drew me in. She acted like she knew exactly what she wanted from me, and I'd be damned if I didn't give it to her.

She cleared her throat, bringing me back from my own mind.

"You can call me Christopher," I continued as she nodded. I sat in my chair and put my arms behind my head. I wanted her to relax, but my lackadaisical approach seemed to make her stiffen even more. She rounded her shoulder and pursed her lips together tightly.

"I am here about Iris and Charles Porter." Her gaze locked on mine, and that pain I'd seen when I first laid eyes on her was more apparent now.

"I'm aware. Scarlett mentioned it. What can an out-of-towner like you want with two dead people?" I asked. I was being an asshole, but every time she opened her mouth, her lips pressed together, their fullness begging to be kissed, I wanted nothing more than to press my lips to hers. I didn't know why I was reacting this way to a stranger. Especially someone who looked like her. I shouldn't want to kiss her. Not now. Not ever.

"Sheriff." Her voice quivered as she moved a little bit closer to my desk.

"Christopher," I reminded her.

"Christopher, then," she replied with a small smile that didn't quite reach her eyes. She gripped the side of my desk with one hand as she continued talking. "Those two dead people, Iris and Charles, were my parents."

Ah, well damn. I am a jerk.

I knew they had a daughter and should have put two and two together, but I was clouded by her looks, her demeanor. Hell, I was distracted by her.

"I am here from Philadelphia to make sure that their murders will be investigated and to offer my services." She stood straighter, releasing the desk.

"I'm very sorry for your loss." I rubbed my cheek with my hand. I shouldn't have been insensitive. I was making light of a situation that I shouldn't have been. I fought back the bile that was churning in my stomach. I had sounded like my father, and he was a man I never wanted to be like

"Thank you." Her tone evened out. "So, what's the plan?"

"Their murders will be investigated but we are a small town. We don't have the resources nor access to the resources you have out where you're from. We are a small team here." I sat up, trying to make myself look and sound more professional. I was pretty sure I'd ruined that.

"All I am asking is that their murders are investigated, impartially."

God, all she wanted was a fair case. For her parents to be treated with the same respect. It sickened me that she even had to ask. I nodded. Questions filled my mind.

"Did you know your grandfather?"

Lillian raised her eyebrows at my question. "You're inter-rogating me now?" She let out a gentle laugh.

"I'm trying to get as much information as possible." I pulled out a piece of paper from my desk and wrote Iris, Charles and Lillian's names. I needed a list of people who knew them. Smack-dab on the top of that list was my father.

"I didn't know my grandfather. I don't know anyone from here at all. My parents had me a few years after moving from Kittrell." She cleared her throat. "We were never welcomed back. Even when my grandfather knew he had a granddaugh-ter."

"I'm sorry." I stopped writing and glanced up at her. "That had to have been tough. Never knowing your family."

"I had all the family I needed in my parents." She fidgeted with the sleeve of her dress.

Now she has no one. No parents or siblings.

"I appreciate your sympathy, but I'd rather you take that sympathy and mold it into something useful. Like action."

I fought back a smile. She told it like it was. I admired that.

"And I'm here at your disposal until this is solved. My boss, Mr. William Harrington, is a prominent lawyer in Phil-adelphia. I have a law degree and can be of assistance."

Her confidence skyrocketed when she spoke about herself. The quiver that had been in her voice disappeared at the men-tion of her law degree.

"You're a lawyer?" Curiosity got the better of me as my mind reeled with even more questions.

I'll be damned.

"Well . . . no, I am not a lawyer." She shifted from leg to leg.

"But you have a law degree?" I asked, confused.

"Yes." She sighed, her eyebrows burrowing together. She looked pointedly at me. "Sometimes that isn't enough. I am a woman . . . a half-black woman at that, if you hadn't noticed,

26

Sheriff. And those things just don't go into the making of a successful lawyer."

I grinned at her and opened my mouth to speak, but she interrupted me.

"Yet."

"I hadn't noticed." Oh, I'd noticed. I noticed everything about her. The almond shape of her eyes and the fullness of her breasts. Her skin. She was all woman.

I shook my head. She was here to solve her parents murder, not to have me drooling over her. I had to stay focused, because if I could give her anything, it'd be her parents murderer. She didn't need a man to guide her through life and be a kept woman.

Finally allowing herself to sit, she crossed her legs, and I tried not to stare at them.

"I assure you that I am useful. You can phone Mr. Harrington and he can speak to who I am. My integrity and qualifications." She leaned closer to me. Her dress became tighter around her chest, accentuating her breasts. I was distracted from her plea and captivated by her beauty. Lillian glanced at me, her eyes quickly diverting from mine. A slight blush crept on her mocha cheeks. She sat back in the chair.

"I know it wouldn't be good for me to be involved in the case directly, but I knew my parents better than anyone here. I want nothing more than to see this solved. And you, I'm sure, do not want the Philadelphia police down here." She crossed her arms over her chest. She was magnificent, even when she was threatening me.

Lillian had come all the way here from Philadelphia on a mission to find out what had happened to her parents, but all she'd done to me over the past ten minutes was to make me want to study every last detail of *her*. That beauty and charm was dangerous. My entire body tingled each time she spoke. Her beauty, her wit, her drive. These were all things that, down here, would make her a target.

What the hell am I going to do to keep her safe?

"No need for me to call Mr. Harrington." I looked at her more closely, her focus never once leaving me. "You will need to stay around anyway, so we can release the bodies to you once they are identified."

She nodded.

"And you will need to make arrangements for a funeral, as well as what will happen to the Porter estate."

"The estate?" she asked, as confusion flitted across her face.

"Yes. Your grandfather had a large estate." I flipped through some paperwork. "Says here it was left to your father. Guess it's yours now."

She frowned and shuffled in her seat. It hurt me to see her so uncomfortable as she didn't seem to know a lot about her family.

"Where are you staying?" I blurted out before I could think better of it. Okay, maybe she could handle herself, but I couldn't send her on her way without making sure she would be safe.

That is part of my job, to keep people safe, right?

She bit slightly on her bottom lip.

"I was planning on getting a room somewhere. I'm not sure where exactly." She sighed and slouched back in the chair. "I honestly hadn't thought that far ahead, but now there's the house you're saying will be mine." She shook her head. "That doesn't matter, though. I can't stay there yet." She shut her eyes momentarily before refocusing on me.

The movement didn't hide the emotion I saw there. The tears that filled her eyes. I rubbed my fingers against the pad of my hand, trying to stop myself from reaching out and telling her I'd make sure everything would be all right.

"My parents stayed there?"

"They did. Their stuff is still there. I haven't had a chance to pack it all up."

"I'll do that eventually. I'm not ready to face that, yet . . ." Her lips curved at the ends in a slight frown, as she hesitated to continue.

I gave Lillian a nod of reassurance that she could say what she needed to say.

"It isn't so much about them staying there, but that I had a family who lived there and didn't care about me or my parents. It's too much heartache for one day, you know?"

All I could do was nod my head again. I didn't know what to say to bring her comfort. I didn't have experience with anything that she was having to deal with, and while I sympathized, I couldn't imagine what it was like to have to run away to be with the one you loved. To be cast out from your family because of that choice. Charles and Iris had dealt with that choice for decades, and when they'd decided to come home, that trip had cost them their lives.

"There's a motel. They will take you." I sucked in a breath at my word choice. Those words made her sound like a burden, and she was far from that. Despite the circumstances that had brought her here, she was a breath of fresh air. Lillian was a woman on a mission who stood up for what she believed in. I could take a few lessons from her.

"I'll take you there for the night. Then tomorrow we can go to the morgue so you can identify the bodies."

Her body language changed. Her eyes glossed over with tears. She had exuded confidence before, but now, she stared down at her feet. I wanted to run and pull her into my arms. To tell her that everything was going to be okay. I squashed that idea. It'd be unprofessional, and well, I was pretty sure she'd smack my stupid ass for putting my hands on her. Or maybe she wouldn't.

"Sherriff, I couldn't impose. I'm sure you have a lot to deal with." She wrung her hands together.

"I insist. Things are different here, Lillian. People don't

take kindly to strangers. Especially strangers that are going to be asking questions and — "

Her eyes widened. She slumped down in the chair further, the exhaustion clearly taking over.

"And look like me," she barely whispered. She shook her head as if not wanting to believe what I was saying.

It hurt me to hear the words just as much as I was sure it hurt her to say them. Kittrell may have been my town, but there were things that we did here that I was not proud of.

"Things are different where I'm from. It isn't as in-your-face."

It.

"That's settled, then. I'll take you. I'll talk to the motel manager and make sure you're all set."

She studied me from under her eyelashes. She was deep in thought, and I was sure she was weighing her options. I knew I was being impulsive, but there was something about her, something that drove me to want to help her. I knew people would talk.

"Okay." She nodded.

"Only if that's what you want, I don't want to push you. I mean . . . I don't know." I didn't want to come over as a man who pushed my ideals down women's throats, because that wasn't my style. I cared about what this woman thought of me.

Lillian grinned at me. And that was it — my nerves disappeared. The smile lit up her face that minutes before had shown the torment and burden of her parent's death.

"Great. Thanks. Christopher," she said my name playfully as she stood then went to exit my office. Her movements were fluid, graceful, and unencumbered.

My body responded to the way she said my name with my blood flowing to my center. I closed my eyes for a second, trying to stay focused on the case and not on how badly I wanted to press my lips against Lillian and show her how much of a gentleman I could be.

"Anytime, Lillian. We will find out who did this. I promise."

She stopped in the doorway, her back still to me. "Lilly," she murmured. "My parents called me Lilly."

"Lilly," I replied, taking the information she had shared about her parents and holding it close. It was just a nickname, but in the little bit of time I'd spoken with Lilly, she hadn't seemed the type to offer stories or nicknames to simply anyone. "Give me a few minutes and I'll take you to the motel. It isn't far from here."

She shut the door behind her, leaving me with the duty of fulfilling the offer that I'd help her find out who had murdered her parents. I would, too. And not because I found her exquisite — although she was definitely one of the finest specimens of a woman I had seen — but because it was my job to keep people safe, to solve crimes. I wasn't supposed to be exerting much effort on this case — when your father was the Mayor, you did as he said. If not . . . Well, I didn't fear for myself anymore. I feared for Lilly.

Chapter Six: Lilly

1937

I quickly shut the door behind me, my heart beating rapidly, and closed my eyes taking a moment to compose myself.

What had I agreed to?

I wasn't an impulsive person. I was rational and thought out each decision I made. But meeting someone like Christopher hadn't even been a thought in my mind when I came to Kittrell, hoping for answers. I guess it was like my mother always told me, *People come into our lives when we least expect it.*

I knew it was Christopher's job to work my parents' case, but when he looked at me, his eyes held something beyond his professional obligation. He'd studied me with an intensity that had me shifting under his gaze. He stared at my lips and my chest. I wasn't uncomfortable, though. I was aroused by the man I'd just met.

My mother had said the first time she met my father it was the same way. That she knew on some level they were destined to be together. I didn't believe in any of that stuff. Okay, well maybe a bit. I mean, what women didn't want that for themselves? I never thought it'd be in the cards for me. My father had always called me strong willed and motivated, which he claimed scared some men. I had never understood why a man would want a woman who only knew how to cook, clean, and pop out babies. I wanted it all.

The differences between Christopher and me were too vast. Plus, I wasn't hoping for anything beyond professional courtesy. I was here to make sure my parents' murderer was caught.

And now, Christopher had to go and offer to take me to a motel and take me to identify my parent's bodies. My head was telling me to do it on my own, to exercise caution, but my body wanted to be sitting across from him while he perused the length of me. Honestly, I had nowhere else to stay, and Christopher was right—this wasn't the kindest town. Oddly, I trusted him. My instincts told me he was sincere and honest in his intentions.

I sat in an old dusty chair thinking about the last few days and how everything had changed so quickly. My parents? Gone. My job? Who knew if I even had a job to go back to? These were things I couldn't control. I had to do what I thought was best. My father had always taught me that. Follow my brain, not my heart, and my brain would never let me down. It was ironic coming from him, because he had followed his heart when it came to my mother. I'd never seen a love quite like my parents'. It was what I admired most about them. In all the years they were together, they had held hands, kissed each other every time they left the house, and always said *I love you.*

I do want that for myself. Someday.

It seemed silly to think about my own love life when my parents had been murdered.

The door creaked just as Christopher stuck his head out.

"Lilly?"

I glanced up at him.

"I'm going to be a few more minutes. I'm sorry. Paperwork is never ending in this job, that's for sure. Scarlett here will get you some coffee while you wait, okay?"

"Thanks. I appreciate all your help, Christopher." My body heated instantly as he looked me over.

"Of course. That's what I'm here for." He tipped his hat as

he securely shut the door. He immediately went back to the telephone, not paperwork as he had mentioned.

It's nothing.

He was probably warning everyone that I was here. Getting people prepared for seeing a new face around for a while.

"Handsome, isn't he?" Scarlett stood in front of me, her hands pressed on her hips. She wore a fire-red dress, black pumps, and she had paired it all with red lipstick. Her outfit was rather brazen and was clearly worn to draw attention. I supposed some women liked that sort of thing.

I had tried so hard to ignore everything about Christopher and chalked up my attraction to my overstimulated mind. Plus, I was focused on my parents. But I had felt it. His stare. I had felt it everywhere. I clenched my thighs together, drops of moisture gathering between my legs. I didn't know if it was sweat from the heat, or my arousal, but I tried to make it go away. I didn't need to blur the lines between business and pleasure. My body, though, was apparently longing for Christopher's eyes again.

I glanced quickly into Christopher's office. He glanced at me, his brown eyes inviting.

Damn that southern hospitality.

It was petrifying. I didn't do instant attraction. I was cautious, and even with friends, I had to get to know them before I'd trust them with anything. Christopher, though, he had pummeled through that wall I had in place, after just one conversation.

He went back to focusing on his phone call, and I allowed myself another second to admire him. His uniform shirt was tight to his body, with rolled up sleeves, and molded to the muscles that ripped down the length of him. Sweat glistened on his forearms — the heat of the southern summer day showing on his body. He removed his hat, then wiped his forehead with the back of his hand.

"I suppose he is handsome." I stood, then moved away

from the view through his office door. I couldn't stop staring at him. Each glance caused a fire to burn in the pit of my stomach. I'd never had that reaction to a man before. Too fast. I couldn't have those feelings—I'd just met the guy. My resolve was dwindling due to the loss of my parents. I was hoping for comfort wherever I could get it. I nodded to myself. That was it.

"Well, you must be blind if you can't see it." Scarlett smacked her lips.

I couldn't figure her out. Her body language made me uneasy. Her very posture commanded and demanded, and yet she seemed innocent enough. The eyes of others glared at us from all over the office, and whispers traveled to my ears. Many of the words were unkind, but some of them were murmurs of curiosity. I wanted to push the words aside and pretend I didn't hear them, but they hurt.

"His dreamy brown eyes and muscles." Scarlett fanned herself with her perfectly manicured hand. "He's spectacular." She leaned in closer, so only I could hear her. "But his father . . . Well, he may be older, but let me tell you . . . I'd be happy to snag any of the Weatherby boys."

"Weatherby boys? There's more than one of them?" I asked, my curiosity getting the better of me.

"Just his father, Mayor Fredrick Weatherby"—she rolled her eyes—"and the sheriff's younger brother, Tucker Weatherby. He's a jerk but has the looks, like his brother. So he has that going for him."

I couldn't help but laugh. Scarlett was a little in-your-face, and clearly infatuated with everything Weatherby, but she was a nice distraction from the thoughts that plagued my mind.

"Where can I get a cup of coffee?" I yawned, the exhaustion finally taking over.

"Oh, I'm sorry. I'm gabbing away." She flung her hands up

in the air dramatically. "Here, let me get it for you. Cream? Sugar?" she asked as she started to walk away.

"Let her get it herself. We don't serve her kind here." A man came up behind us, and we both turned towards him. The whispers from before were one thing, just people buzzing by and mumbling under their breath. This man, though, he wanted me to know the hatred spewing from his lips was his, and his alone.

"Speak of the devil," Scarlett said softly. "Tucker, this is Ms. Porter. She's here about her parent's murder."

I extended my hand to him, deciding to take the higher ground. He glanced down at my outstretched hand as if I had some incurable disease. Jerk was not the only word that came to my mind as I stood there, arm extended, left looking like an idiot. Everyone in the office had stopped to view our exchange, and I had to talk myself down from telling him where to go and how to get there. It wasn't very ladylike and wouldn't make a good first impression.

I pulled back my hand as someone walked past, murmuring, "Half-breed," just loud enough so I could hear it. Tucker smiled, and my body broke out in goosebumps. There was something unsettling about him. Something that made me slightly uneasy. It was amazing to me that Christopher and Tucker were brothers. The instant comfort I had felt with Christopher was far from my first impression of Tucker. If he wanted to be an asshole, I wouldn't be a docile girl hiding behind fear of what others would think.

"My apologies, Tucker." I enunciated his name. "Where I'm from, it's common courtesy to shake hands when you meet someone."

Scarlett chuckled next to me, and Tucker gave her a pointed stare that quickly shut her up.

"Well, here, where I'm from, I don't have to shake hands with niggers."

The office was silent. The hustle and whispers were gone. You could hear a pin drop, and at that moment, I'd take the pin dropping to clear the tension in the air. I had to say something, stand my ground and let him know that I couldn't and wouldn't stand for that abuse. I was treading on tricky territory, so I had to choose my words carefully.

"Ignorance is unfortunate. I would agree, however," I said as I still tried to make my point. "I'm not sure I see any of that around here."

"You fucking—"

The door swung open and Christopher came out, interrupting Tucker's tirade.

"I see you met my brother Tucker." He smacked his brother on the shoulders, the scowl never leaving Tucker's face.

"I did," I said politely.

Christopher stopped and looked between us, the tension boiling over. Something clicked in his eyes as he furrowed his brow. This simple motion accentuated his facial features, and I found myself thinking that indeed Scarlett was right. Christopher was handsome. He was tanned from the southern sun, and now that I could clearly see the full length of him, he had an athletic body.

"All right everyone, back to work!" Christopher yelled, as people stole glances and milled about.

"Did you need something, Tucker?" Scarlett asked.

"No, I came to see if my brother wanted to go to lunch, but I see he has other plans." He eyeballed me.

"I do. I'm taking Lilly to David's motel to get settled." Christopher barely made eye contact with his brother as he put his hand on the small of my back, signifying his readiness to go. "Shall we?"

Tucker stood staring at me and his brother. Our closeness wasn't anything. It wasn't a kiss, it wasn't anything crazy, but the gesture, his hand touching my body, must have meant something more to Tucker than even I could fathom. He stomped away, mumbling something about having a talk with his father.

"I'm sorry," I said to Christopher as we exited the station.

"For what?" he asked.

"It seemed tense in there between you and your brother." I tried to use my words carefully. I didn't know Christopher, and while I felt I could trust him, I was also cautious. "I know that things are different here. Separate but equal. Whatever that means. But if you helping me beyond what you should is going to cause trouble, I can get around myself." I paused, not knowing what else to say.

We reached his truck, and Christopher opened the door for me. Another gesture I was not used to being afforded. I sat, waiting for him to get in the vehicle. When he finally did, we were in silence for a moment, just staring out the windows.

"Listen, Lilly." Christopher had a way about him. A way in which he commanded my attention. He reminded me a lot of my father. "My family is racist. I'm not going to lie. That's how I was raised. Hate. Violence. All of it."

I wrung my hands together. Not out of nervousness, but out of not knowing what else to do. He was being candid with me. So open. While I appreciated that, I didn't quite know where this conversation was headed.

"That's not who I am. That's never been who I am. I'm twenty-six years old and I have never once stood up to my old man about what I believe in. Now I have this case and it seems like I could make a difference. I think it's about time that things change, don't you?" He smiled at me.

I appreciated the sentiment and his desire for change, but I couldn't help but wonder, why now? Why all of a sudden was he jumping to make a difference when he had stayed quiet before?

"I am thankful for you helping me, but I don't want to be a pawn in some endeavor you have to get back at your father. I'm here to get justice."

"I know. We can help each other. Isn't that what friends do?" He turned to face me, and his grin was returning. The one that made me weak at the knees yet screamed Christopher was nothing but trouble.

"Friends? We just met each other. I'm not sure how we can be classified as friends."

Christopher laughed. "Maybe in Philadelphia there's a time limit before you can be friends, but in the South, everyone's a friend." He patted my leg. "Plus, I like your spunk, Lilly. I like that you came all the way out here for what you believe in, and that you didn't cower down to my brother." He paused. "So yes, I think we are friends, don't you?"

With that response, I couldn't help but nod in agreement.

Friends.

I suppose my silence sufficed for an answer, because before I could say anything else, he started his truck and we were on our way to the motel. I was happy that Christopher accepted me. I worried about everyone else.

CHAPTER SEVEN: CHRISTOPHER

1937

We pulled up to the motel, and I rushed to try and help Lilly from the car. Before I could even make to open her door, she was out and trying to drag her suitcases from the back seat. Any other woman I'd been around would have waited and expected me to not only open the door for her but to take her bags. Lilly was far from any other woman. She screamed independence, and it drew me that much more to her.

"I can get that." I went behind her, reached around, our fingers brushing when I took her bag. She might have screamed independence, but I was a southern gentleman through and through, and my mother would have keeled over in her grave knowing that I hadn't helped Lilly with her bags. My hardened shaft was right up against the fabric of her dress. I wasn't sure she would notice it, with all that damn fabric around her, but her breath hitched in her throat.

Her hands were soft, much softer than I imagined they'd be. She was distant and protective of herself, so her softness took me off guard.

"Thanks."

I caught a blush to her cheeks as she held her hand close to her chest. I lifted her bags out, my breath touching against her neck. I watched her caress where my breath had just touched.

So, she had felt it.

I mentally berated myself for thinking, yet again, about

Lilly in a romantic way. She was here because she needed to bury her parents. She needed to find out who murdered them in cold blood. But I couldn't help but be drawn to everything about her. The way she smelt like freshly picked flowers, the tenacity in her voice when she spoke about her parents and about the justice that needed to be served.

"This way." I led the way to the motel office. Lilly made sure to walk away from me, the distance between us uncomfortable. I was glad to open the door to the motel and get out of the heat. The doorbell rang when I entered, and the silence went away with it. A radio played in the background and a waft of cool air hit me from the fan. It was refreshing, because I was hot and frustrated for a variety of reasons.

"Hello?" I called out. Lilly came up beside me.

"This feels heavenly," she said closing her eyes and taking in the coolness of the air as it surrounded her.

I took the opportunity to look at her. Not just her face, which shined with sweat, or the plumpness of her lips that she licked as she enjoyed the fan, but her figure.

"It is." I thought these words were only in my head, but apparently my mouth had betrayed me.

Lilly opened her eyes as she sucked in a sharp breath. She obviously knew I was talking about more than the fan. While I should have searched for something to say to clear the air, I didn't. I held her gaze until a clearing of a throat brought us back from the moment.

"Sheriff." David, the owner of the motel smiled at Lilly and me.

I shook my head, trying to refocus on getting Lilly settled. "Ms. Porter here would like a room."

David nodded and took a key out of the cabinet.

Lilly riffled through her bag. "How much, sir?"

"Nothing," David said confidently. "Any friend of the Sheriff is a friend of mine."

David was an older man, old enough to be my grandfather. He walked with a cane and should have been at home in his rocking chair instead of running this place. His grandson, Matthew, helped him keep the place up, when he wasn't out causing trouble. Getting into trouble seemed to be more his thing lately.

"Thank you, Sir, but . . ."

David put up his hand. "David. Call me David," he said with a toothless grin. "Let me do this for you."

Lilly smiled back at him. "I appreciate it. How about I return after I get settled, and we have some sweet tea together?"

"That sounds mighty nice." David handed Lilly her key.

I felt a ping of jealousy that David would get to spend time with Lilly, and I wouldn't. I pushed it aside as we walked to her room. I had to do my job, solve her parents murder. That was my number one priority.

"Home sweet home." I opened the door to the room then dropped her bags. Lilly walked right in then sat on the bed that took up the majority of the room. I stayed back, hovering by the door. I wasn't sure what to do. My body ached to be near this woman I had only met hours before, but my mind replayed her mother's brutalized body over and over again — the lashes, Charles reaching out for her even in death. Any feelings for Lilly would only lead to trouble. Trouble was something we already had enough of.

"You can sit." Lilly motioned to the tattered chair that was over in the corner.

I thought about it some more. Sit. Don't sit. Talk. Don't talk. These choices left me feeling as though I'd be in the wrong with one of them. "I can't."

Her face contorted into a frown, and I saw tears filling her eyes. Just as quick as her faced changed, she sat straighter and brought her hands into her lap.

"Hey." I moved nearer to her, and the door closed behind

me. "It's not you. It's me." I winced. Not what I wanted to say. "I have to work. They're expecting me back at the station."

She nodded and stood, opening the door to the outside. She brushed past me, as if I meant nothing, as if the words I said had hurt her.

"Thank you, Sheriff. I'll see you in the morning, around eight?" Lilly was back to business.

"Yes, to go to the morgue and identify your parents." I stepped out the door. "Rest well, Lilly."

"You too, Sheriff." And with a gentle shut of the door, Lilly was gone.

"Idiot," I mumbled to myself. I slid back into my truck and listed all the things I had done wrong. I should have stayed, even for a few minutes. Lilly had no one here. She was smack-dab in the middle of one of the most racist towns around, and I had obviously made her think she was worthless. She wasn't worthless. I knew that she was worth much more than this life was willing to give her, yet I couldn't bring myself to let her know she was more than a woman looking for justice where it just wouldn't be found.

Chapter Eight: Charles

1907

I sat up in my bed and looked down, watching Iris through the window. She was humming. I couldn't hear the tune, but the little purse of her lips and the slight sway of her hips were her signature moves for when she was focused and in song. The impending sunrise with its orangey-yellow hue peeked out of the horizon. I had never appreciated the sun. It rose and fell every day, and I had never paid much attention to. But here, now, as it reflected off Iris' pale-yellow dress, kissing her skin as it danced across her face, the world seemed different. It held a beauty I'd never seen before.

I was scared. Not because of some foolish rules, but because every time she was near me, my heart hitched in my chest and strangled my throat. Which was precisely why I couldn't talk to her.

"You can talk to her, yanno?"

I jumped then spun around. Virginia was standing in the doorway with her hands on her hips. She was like my mother, raising me since I was a baby.

"I—"

Virginia chuckled.

I couldn't lie. Not to Virginia. "I don't know what to say." I glanced out the window again as Iris hung sheets on the clothesline.

"Charles, from the moment you were born you haven't stayed quiet. You know what you want to say. You're a man

44

now. Eighteen years old."

Truth was I couldn't decide what I wanted to say. I wanted to tell her she was the most wonderful thing I'd ever seen. That since I met her nothing else mattered. Not thoughts of college, not the other girls who'd been pining for me to court them, nor my life that had been planned since before I was born. None of it mattered as much as she did to me. Since that day she had shoved her hand in my face and made me shake it.

"What if she doesn't like me?"

Now, my fears were showing. It wasn't that Iris and I could both be hung for our affections for one another — it was that she might not feel the same about me. As far as I was concerned, that fear was love in its truest form.

"You won't know unless you ask."

I watched Virginia leave before scurrying about my room, throwing on clothes to head out to talk with Iris. The house was asleep, my father likely still passed out from a night of cigars and drinking. Fredrick wouldn't be over until well past noon trying to find me. Now was my chance.

I walked out into the backyard. Iris wasn't facing me as she continued to hum and sway her luscious hips. I thought about wrapping my hands around her waist and pulling her close against me, something I'd wanted to do for a while now. I had watched many men take their workers whenever they wanted, but I didn't want that. I needed her to love me. To want me like I wanted her.

"Iris?" My voice was just above a whisper as she turned around, a smile stretching across her face.

"Do you need something, sir?" She placed the rest of the clothes in the basket, then focused on me.

The thing about Iris was she really looked at you. She was good at reaching into the recesses of your soul and pulling out all your insecurities, your doubts, your fears. Right now, she held my desires.

"Charles. I want you to call me Charles."

She nodded before taking another item of clothing from the basket.

"Do you want to go to the lake with me?" I blurted out. Fredrick and I had taken many girls there, but something about sharing that place with Iris made me sweaty and nervous. There, we could be alone. I wouldn't have to sneak out to talk to her before the sun rose.

"I can't. I've got work to do."

A clearing of the throat shifted our focus.

"I'll finish the clothes, baby. You go with Charles."

Virginia winked at me, and I wanted to run over and kiss her face. Iris hesitated and shifted her feet as she glanced between her mother and me.

"Okay." She smoothed out her dress before coming beside me.

We walked to the lake, silence the only topic of conversation. I wanted to ask her so many questions. Where had she been before? Why was she separated from her mother? Did she think about me like I thought about her?

When we finally made it to the lake, Iris stood still, staring off into the distance. I looked at her, the lake reflecting in the green of her eyes.

"How'd you get such beautiful eyes?"

"I don't know." She blushed. "Maybe my father. I never knew who he was."

"Oh." I sat and picked nervously at the ground. Iris sat next to me, stretching out her long legs in front of her.

"I barely knew my mother until your father brought me on to work. I was raised by my aunt in South Carolina. I got a decent education. Learned to read and write properly enough then brought here to be with my mother once I was old enough to be of service."

A lump formed in my throat. My father may have not bought her but there was no very little difference in my eyes. I knew they weren't paid fair wages. To my father, Iris was nothing more than a centerpiece at our already overflowing table.

"You aren't a servant to me, Iris. You are a regular person." I reached out and gripped her hand. The touch wasn't meant to be romantic. It was just that I needed to feel her, to hold her tight, and to let he know I was serious. "I like you," I added.

She laughed and took her hand away. "Charles, you don't know me." She continued staring off at the lake. "I'm a black girl with no future other than a world of hanging clothes and constantly looking over my shoulder, wondering what will happen next." She took a deep breath.

Her confession was heart breaking. Sure, I didn't know everything about her, but I knew what mattered most. "I know when you laugh, you get carried away and snort a little. You can't cook for the dickens and Virginia often has to throw away a loaf of bread because you burn it so badly."

Iris' chest rose and fell dramatically, but she still focused ahead.

"When you hang clothes to dry, you hum and sway your hips to a beat that only you can hear." The wind found us, freeing a stray piece of her hair. I tucked it behind her ear and continued as she slowly turned to face me. "And I know that you are the most beautiful person that I've ever seen."

Iris tilted her head to the side, studying my face. I didn't know why I took it as an invitation, but I did, leaning in slowly and brushing my lips against hers. She lifted her arms, grasping my biceps and holding me firmly against her. There were no tongues, no groping, nor anything else of that sort. Just our lips, forbidden, swollen and filled with need, pressing against one another's.

We broke apart, Iris quickly turning her head to stare out

at the lake again. I smiled, the unease slowly lifting from inside me. I knew what I felt for Iris was something real and this kiss sealed it for me. Despite what our relationship could mean, I was calm, happy, and hopeful.

"I like you, too."

Those words were everything to me. I glanced up, the sun firmly placed in the sky, high, bright, and shining down on Iris and me. Our confessions, our stolen kiss, held the promise of something great. Something that would change the world, no matter how difficult it might be.

Taking her hand in mine again, we stayed that way, for as long as we could without raising suspicion. Relishing in the moment, the unspoken words of our future together. Our future was bright, like the sun that shone down on us, showing us the beauty in the world. Iris and I were soulmates, and nothing would come between us.

CHAPTER NINE: LILLY

1937

Why did I care whether Christopher stayed or left? He owed me nothing and was already going above and beyond by helping me find a place to sleep and taking me around. Christopher could have pointed to the nearest motel and sent me on my way. Yet he hadn't. He'd driven me. He'd opened doors for me. He'd taken my bags and made me feel like I was beautiful. And it annoyed me.

I wasn't a believer in fairy tales. I was a believer in hard work, perseverance, and independence. There was something that I couldn't shake when Christopher was close to me. Shockwaves had gone through my body when our fingers brushed and threatened all those beliefs I had.

I lay on the bed and closed my eyes. Sleep came right away, the day of travel finally catching up with me. It wasn't a dreamless sleep. It was filled with him—Christopher.

It was snap-shots, slow moving pictures of him grinning, his muscles rippling against his uniform. Even in my sleep, I felt aroused, my thighs clenching together, wetness pooled at my center. It was a blissful dream. No hesitation, no confusion in his eyes. Just want. Just need.

I woke up as the clock turned four in the afternoon and I headed back to the motel reception—the promise of sweet tea cooling my overheated body.

The bell rang when I opened the door, and David was already waiting at the small table in the front office. He had changed from his tattered jeans and T-shirt to wearing a pair of nice slacks and a button-up shirt. I fought back a smile at his hair. He was almost bald, except for a small patch that he had combed over.

"I wondered when you'd show!" He struggled to get up, and I thought about running to help him. I didn't, though. He clearly didn't want help. He wanted to do it all on his own, and I respected that. Even with his own struggles, David held out the chair for me.

"Sit." He motioned to the chair. I sat as he fought to push in my chair. I may have moved my feet a bit to help him. Christopher had warned me about this town, but I wasn't uncomfortable with David. He seemed genuine, unplagued by the hate.

"I took a nap. It was a long day of traveling." I rolled my neck, remembering the hard train seats as David handed me a glass of sweet tea. Condensation dripped from the glass onto my hands as I sipped the deliciousness. It brought temporary solace from the humidity as it sizzled on my hot skin.

"So, pretty lady. Tell me what brings you to our town? Your parents? "

I placed my glass down. The need to talk to someone overwhelmed me.

"Or is it the Sheriff? He is quite the catch. And single." He winked at me.

Heat gathered in my cheeks at the mention of the Sheriff.

"You're smitten for sure." He shook his head.

"I met him today, David," I said with a frown.

"I met my wife at the county fair. She came to my booth and wanted to try to play the ring toss game."

I stared at him in confusion.

"You know, where you throw the ring and try to get it around the base of the milk bottle?"

I nodded.

"Well, she lost. Bad." He laughed. "I gave her a prize anyway. She was beautiful. The sun in my sky."

"What happened to her?"

"She passed a few years back. Got the cancer." He took a sip of his drink. "So, Ms. Lilly, love can happen right away. Cause she winked at me and boy, I was in love. I courted her two months before I asked her to marry me."

I snorted. "I'm not the marrying type. I'm too strong willed."

"Sherriff likes the strong-willed types. That's what he needs. Not a Scarlett."

My interest was piqued at the mention of Scarlett. I knew I'd sensed something with her when I met her. She had probably thought I was after the Sheriff. There was a huge difference between us. I glanced down at my caramel skin. A difference that had got my own parents killed due to how they felt about each other.

"Other than denying you like the Sheriff, I'm sorry about your parents." He stared down at his drink.

"They were great parents. Someone thought that because they came back here, to where my father was from and my mother a servant, that they could take their lives because they loved each other." I paused as I fought back the tears. "It's wrong."

"Ah, hell, sweet thang. I'm sorry. Ain't no one deserve to have their life taken." He reached out and squeezed my hand tightly before releasing it. "I don't care about the color of your skin or how much money you have hidden under your mattress. We all get buried in the ground and rot." David's words were harsh but true.

"You're right. If only everyone thought like you." I played with the ice in my glass.

"Now that would be a scary world." He wiggled his white eyebrows.

We talked for hours. David was a firm believer in loving who you wanted and living your life.

"If they're nice to me, I'll be nice to them. I don't care what they look like."

"Thank you, David. I enjoyed our talk." I placed a kiss to his cheek. "And the sweet tea, but I'm extremely tired."

He opened the door for me. "Anytime, pretty lady. It's not often an old man like me gets company." Although naturally slumped in the shoulders due to his old age, he straightened them as much as he could.

"Get into your room now Miss. Lilly. Lock that door tight."

I glanced behind me and saw shadows in the trees that surrounded the motel. A few men where whistling, and I saw their shadows circling about. My back went rigid.

"Don't mind them. I may be old, but I ain't no push over. I stand up for what's right." He leaned in, grabbed my hand and placed a gentle kiss on it. The noises from the men in the woods got louder and louder. I glanced over my shoulder again, light from torches was dancing on the trees and illuminating the sky. It would have been beautiful had I known they weren't here to cause harm.

"Damn bastards!" David called out to the woods.

I shook my head. I wouldn't leave him to deal with whatever these crazy men were thinking of doing. I knew they were only here because David had opened his motel to me.

"I'll be staying here with you, David." I went back inside the office then shut the door, locking it behind us.

David stared at me for a moment, but he didn't protest. He went to the small kitchen area that was off the office and made us some food. We both sat at the table, barely talking, listening to the sounds of the night, and the radio softly playing.

Suddenly, the quiet was replaced with hooting, hollering, and the sound of gun shots. David claimed the noise was a bad engine, a car backfiring. I might have been a city girl, but

I knew better.

"Damn nigger lover!"

Pounding at the door made me jump. David kept on humming a tune that was on the radio, seemingly unfazed by what was happening.

I didn't sleep a wink that night. Although David put up a tough front, he didn't either. We sat and we listened to the threats of violence and to words that I'd never heard spoken before. I heard the hate. My parents had told me stories about what they had had to endure. It was different to be living it, hearing it spoken to you. My body tingled with fear. Part of me wanted to see these men face-to-face and tell them all how wrong they were for what they were doing—the other part, the one who knew what people were capable of, was afraid.

Chapter Ten: Christopher

1937

I had wanted to stay with Lilly. I had promised her that I'd figure out what happened to her parents, but I couldn't do that by sitting in her motel room trying not to think about what I would give to kiss her. Normally, reacting this way to a woman wasn't an issue. Lilly, though, wasn't a woman I should have been interested in, and my attraction to her threatened everything our society had been built on. I had to focus.

I pulled up to the mayor's home. I found my father sitting on the back porch with a drink in his hand.

"Tough day at the office?" I asked, pulling up a chair then sitting across from him.

He ignored my question as he took another sip of his drink. "I'd offer you a drink, but I know you aren't here on a pleasure visit." He set his drink down. "What do you want, Christopher?"

"I want to know about Iris and Charles." I grabbed my notepad. "Any ideas who'd want them dead?"

"Seriously? I thought I said put your minimal into this case. Asking me questions isn't going to get you anywhere."

I tapped my finger on my notepad trying to keep myself calm. "Father, you knew them both."

"Over 30 years ago!" He shook his head. "People change, Christopher."

I doubted that Iris and Charles had been the same people

they were all those years ago, but someone had a grudge and had been waiting for them. Something told me that my father might have a clue who that person was.

"Tell me about when you met Iris. What was she like?"

My father sighed. I got my persistence from him. He knew I wouldn't stop asking until I received an answer.

"If I tell you this, will you leave me alone?"

I nodded. And he began his story.

"Charles, why are you dragging me to meet some servant girl."

Charles' eyes sparkled with something I wasn't sure how to de-scribe it. Putting his hands on my shoulders, his gaze found mine.

"She's different, Fredrick. She's got a passion, a drive that I'm not familiar with. And her eyes." He smiled "The brightest green eyes . . ."

I frowned. "Sounds like you like her."

We continued to walk into the woods and down to the lake.

"I do," Charles said confidently.

There wasn't any hesitation and his forthrightness startled me. What was he thinking?

"I get it. You want to have sex with her.". Charles and I were both getting older; it was only a matter of time before sex became our focus. At almost 17, I had yet to meet a person that made me want that exclusively with them

Charles stopped. "No." He glared at me. "It's more than that."

I began to panic. More than what? Sex? I shook my head. No. No. No. That wasn't allowed.

"Iris." Charles' hostile tone of voice from moments ago changed as we came upon the lake.

There she sat, his Iris, the girl who was, "more than that". I guess I saw the draw to her. She had full lips, and her skin was smooth and flawless, and I knew then that Charles was going to make a decision that would impact his life forever. He was in love with that girl. Something in me stirred, too. In the pit of my stomach, like a thou-sand butterflies fluttering.

"I'm Iris." She held her hand out to me.

Charles begged me with his eyes to shake her hand, to give her a chance. Giving Iris a chance, shaking her hand was against everything I'd been taught. Everything that I knew to be the way things were. She shoved her hand closer and Charles grinned. She was passionate. He was right. I found myself shaking her hand, sitting with them at the lake, and eating sandwiches and laughing. It all seemed normal. For those hours that we spent together — that the world around us would have scowled at — all the hate seemed idiotic and unnecessary.

Then, my father's voice came into my mind. He was molding me into his follower. Into a man bred from the same cloth, a man who embraced the ideology that was running through the world like water and from which everyone was drinking.

The time ended. Iris went back to work in the kitchen and Charles went about pretending he didn't think loving a woman like her was forbidden. And I? I kept their secret. Why? I'd never know. Maybe it was her eyes. Maybe it was the way she made me shake her hand without words. Maybe it was the feeling I got in my stomach when she looked at me. Maybe it was her.

It was like I was there, sitting by the lake watching them all become friends. I was more confused than ever. I pressed for more information, but my father mumbled something about a meeting and ran off. This story seemed intertwined, and that there was possibly more to it than what I had originally realized. I needed more information, but I had no idea where to go to get it. It was time to go home and start afresh in the morning.

I pulled up to my house and walked into the sound of Virginia's yelling.

"Mud. Everywhere!"

"What's wrong Virginia?"

Virginia was my housekeeper. She was more than that,

though. She was my mother when mine hadn't been able to care for me. She was my friend when I needed someone to talk to. When my father became mayor, I took over our family home, which meant Virginia and Jeremiah had stayed. Things were different now, but Virginia though, she stuck close to me.

"Someone tracked mud in here with their damn boots, and I've been cleaning it up for the past two days." She mumbled some other words under her breath as she continued scrubbing the kitchen floor on her hands and knees.

"Mud?" I bent down and picked up some of the mud in my hands. "Who was here Virginia? Where did this mud come from?"

She eyed me and threw the sponge in the bucket. This looked like the same mud from the woods with its pink hue and grainy nature. That was why everyone hated that area so much, the pink tint made it a pain to clean up as it was sticky and clumped together.

"I don't know, Christopher. If I did, I'd beat them with this damn sponge!" She gathered the bucket, creaked open the back door, and a slosh of water hit the grass.

Other than myself, Jeremiah, and Tucker were usually the only ones who wore boots in this house. Jeremiah had been raised by Virginia too, so we had grown up like brothers.

Jeremiah and Tucker weren't capable of killing Iris and Charles Porter. They couldn't be. My brother was an asshole, but violent? And Jeremiah, he'd never so much as raised his voice. But I had learned over the past few days, hate could make people do some crazy things.

I went into the closet where all the shoes were kept. Every single pair of boots had mud on them, including my own.

"Damn!" I said aloud. This one possible lead was taking me in circles. Not only because it was such a small hunch, but because I was sure that if I went into every closet in this town right now, there would be muddy boots.

I stormed up the stairs and headed to the room where Tucker usually stayed when he decided to come around. I banged on the door.

"What?" he called out as I opened the door without an invitation.

"Were you at the crime scene?" I held his muddy boots in my hand.

He just glared at me — a crazy *I don't care what you think you know* look.

"I don't know. Ask Jeremiah. He borrowed my boots when we had that bad rainstorm. Maybe he was at the crime scene." Tucker kept smiling as he leaned back on his bed and closed his eyes.

I slammed the bedroom door then clenched my fists at my side. Virginia met me on the landing.

"You're trailing mud!" She shooed me away.

"Virginia? Iris and Charles Porter . . . You knew them, didn't you?" It was a stupid question — I knew she had. She had worked for Charles' parents before being sold off to my father.

"Of course, I knew them." She avoided my eyes.

I wasn't accustomed to seeing her like that. Like Lilly, she was a strong woman, and seeing her nervousness piqued my interest.

"Can you tell me anything about them? I'm running into a whole lot of nothing. And their daughter is in town, and I want to help her." I rubbed my face.

"Their daughter?" Virginia dropped the broom then wiped her hands on her apron.

"Yes. Lillian." I smiled. "Or Lilly, as she likes to be called. She's something, that's for sure."

Virginia went as white as a ghost and excused herself due to feeling ill.

I didn't know what was with everyone today. They were all avoiding my questions. I sighed, resolving that I'd have to deal with the tension and avoidance that had taken over everyone in the morning.

I headed down the corridor to my room to finally get some sleep, but Jeremiah was standing at the end of the landing waiting for me.

"You know I didn't hurt those people."

I nodded and hoped that it would give reassurance as I moved into my room. My feet were heavy with each step I made. Everything had overwhelmed me at once.

CHAPTER ELEVEN: CHRISTOPHER

1937

I had a bit more energy, thanks to a decent night's sleep. In no small part to the fact that I was going to see Lilly again, I had also recovered my determination. After the night before and the damn muddy boots, I had taken a step back and tried to rationalize the evidence. Honestly, everyone had muddy boots. This past week had been a barrage of rainstorm after rainstorm. I also felt guilty for thinking Tucker was capable of murder, but I couldn't disregard anyone. I even questioned my own father's motives and potential involvement.

I was taking Lilly to identify her parents' bodies, not the happiest of occasions, but I hadn't been able to get her out of my mind after things had died down last night. Her smile, her laugh. Everything about her had drawn me in since I'd first laid eyes on her. I had walked down the steps yesterday at the office, and my whole world had changed.

"Lilly?" I knocked on her motel door. No answer. I figured she was in the shower or something, so I knocked and knocked some more until I finally took the hint that maybe she wasn't there and headed to the office. David had probably conned her into coffee this morning, too.

I pushed the office door. It was locked. "Hello?" I banged my fists on the wooden door. It was business hours and the door should have been open.

"Christopher?"

I banged again just as I heard my name.

"It's me, Lilly. Open up," I jiggled the doorknob. "Why is the door locked?" I began to panic. What the hell happened?

I heard the lock clank, and Lilly stood before me in the same clothes she had been wearing the previous day. I peered inside and watched David trying to get up.

"It's okay, David. You can stay where you are." I hovered over the table, and David huffed and stayed seated.

"Someone care to tell me why you both were locked away in here?"

"Oh, it was nothing at all." Lilly began fidgeting and clearing the wooden table. The rotted surface was littered with empty cups and half-eaten food.

"From the looks of it, you and David were holed up here all night."

"Seems your eyes are still working," David muttered, ignoring my earlier suggestion and finally getting up from the chair. "I'm going to bed. I'll let Lilly explain." David hobbled away.

I watched Lilly for a few minutes. Worry settled in my stomach like a dead weight as she tried to keep busy by cleaning up the table.

"Stop watching me. You're making me nervous." Lilly laughed softly as she turned towards me.

"Are you going to tell me what happened here?" I folded my arms across my chest.

Lilly moved her gaze down to my arms, but then quickly darted it away.

I knew she was hoping I hadn't noticed. Oh, but I'd noticed, and I gave those hard-earned muscles a little squeeze for good measure. I fought back a smile as she took a deep breath.

"It was nothing. Just some guys waiting outside when I went to leave. I didn't want to leave David in here all alone, so I stayed."

I moved closer to her. She bit on her lip, but this was the only sign that she wasn't telling the whole truth. That she was probably downplaying what happened.

"Lilly." I growled her name.

The nervous movements she'd been displaying a minute earlier were gone as she stared me down. Her large green eyes bore into me. Their intensity was unsettling, and quite honestly, I was a little afraid of her.

"Don't Lilly me. They came here clearly ready for trouble, shooting off their guns—"

"Jesus," I interrupted.

Lilly held up her hand to stop me from talking.

"This is going to happen, Christopher. People are going to do stupid things because I'm here. I didn't want David to get harassed because of me. They're all bark and no bite." She smiled. "See," she said, and she held up her hands so I could get a good look at her. "I'm fine."

"You're fine, but your parents aren't. Your parents were killed by folk like those outside last night."

She gasped at my words and stumbled back.

I was being insensitive, but I had to impress upon her how important safety was at all times. "So, don't think that you're invincible. You aren't. And David . . . he knows the risk of voicing his disapproval and all that other garbage. This isn't the first time he's been targeted."

Lilly sat in the chair, the realization of my words clearly hitting her.

"His cane," she stated, and I nodded.

"As a teenager, he protected a young black girl from a group of young white men. His repayment was two broken legs, a collapsed lung, and the permanent need for the cane."

Lilly brought her hand to her mouth. "David was calm last night," Lilly said. "Like it didn't faze him."

"He may be old, but he's no pushover," I said proudly.

David's motel was where Tucker and I had come to play when we were younger. He had taken care of me and taught me how wrong the hate that ran through our town was. He had taught me how to be a man.

"He said the same," Lilly said as she stood then moved towards the door. "I'm going to take a shower and change out of yesterday's clothes. If you'd still be willing to take me to the morgue to identify the bodies?" She was back to business again. Conversations were always hot and cold with this woman.

"Yes, that's why I came here."

She hesitated at the door for a minute. That's wasn't the only reason I was here. I knew it. And from the way Lilly glanced at me, she knew it too.

"I didn't know if maybe you could come with me to my room. After last night, I'm still a bit unnerved." She didn't make eye contact with me when she made her request. I knew it took a lot for her to ask, so I tried to be as professional as possible.

"Of course."

As we went to leave, Matthew, David's grandson burst through the door. He was covered in sweat. Lilly jumped in reaction, and I motioned for her to go to her room. She nodded and scurried away.

"Sheriff." Matthew looked at the floor as he moved into the office.

"What'd you do last night Matthew?" I caught the back of his shirt and forced him down into a chair. He had turned sixteen and was running with the wrong crowd. I knew it, everyone knew it. He was coming in, and from his blood shot eyes and disheveled appearance, he had clearly been up all night.

"I was with some friends." He picked his fingernails.

"Right." I pulled back a chair and sat next to him. "Friends that came to spook your grandfather and Ms. Porter?"

He shifted in his seat.

"Don't lie to me Matthew. I can haul you in for disturbing the peace."

"No, don't!" He sat straighter. "Don't tell Grandpa, okay?"

I leaned back in the chair. Now we were getting somewhere.

"I wanted to see what it was like, to go with them. They wanted to make her leave and scare my grandpa from helping other niggers."

I slapped the back of his head. "That's not what they are. They're people. They have names, and jobs, and families."

Matthew nodded.

I sounded like some equal opportunity picketer. I fought back a smile. I liked the sound of me sticking up for what I believed in.

"Lilly's parents were murdered. You know that, right?"

"Yes." He had resorted to picking his nails again.

I sighed. Matthew was lost. This town had been fucking boring when I was a teenager. If it hadn't been for joining the police department, I'd probably have gone down the same path.

"Want to share who else was involved?"

Matthew shot up from his chair, letting it tip back and slam against the wall.

"No way, Sheriff. I saw what they can do. I don't want to get hurt." He paced up and down.

I stood then moved towards him, placing my hand on his shoulder. "I'll protect you, son. Tell me."

He shook his head. "Tell my grandpa if you have to, but they will hurt me, and him, and anyone else that don't believe what they do." The look in his eyes was pure fear.

"It's okay," I reassured him. He needed to settle down, get his head right. "Listen, go get some rest, and I'll be back once

I'm done with Lilly, and we can talk some more. I can protect you and your grandfather. I promise."

He nodded and walked away.

I didn't know what I was getting myself into by offering to protect him. I knew I could. But everywhere I turned, I saw people chatting and waving at me, and any one of them could be behind all this. That was the most difficult thing—I wasn't sure what I could do about it.

I hoped that when I came back from the morgue with Lilly, Matthew would talk to me. I wanted to let the information I'd shared with him stew, and maybe then he would tell me who was here with him last night.

I made my way to Lilly's room. I tried to turn the knob and grinned when I couldn't turn it. I knocked, and Lily opened the door, leaving the deadbolt still locked. Acknowledging it was me, she smiled before letting me in.

"Everything okay?" Lilly asked with concern as I made my way into her room.

Being in this room with her was intimate. I'd been with women, but none had made me feel vulnerable and more in tune with myself, quite like Lilly had.

"Yeah, Matthew, David's grandson, was there last night and is scared of what will happen to him or his grandpa if he tells me who else was with him."

I didn't know what I expected Lilly to say, but she was calm and nodded. "I get it. I hope he finds the courage to come forward with information."

I was stunned at her demeanor. I wanted to beat the information out of Matthew, and I didn't have a personal investment in this case like she did.

"Make yourself at home. I'll try to be quick." Lilly opened the closet then took a dress out.

I sat in the chair and watched her. I was mesmerized by the way she moved, deliberate, but with a grace that captivated me. Every movement of her body had a purpose. It was magnetic and I was stuck.

Lilly went into the bathroom and left the door ajar, I assumed for the steam to escape. From the angle of the chair I sat in I could see an outline on the wall. The door obstructed my view of her, but, as she undressed the shadow danced. I cursed the door, but then as she moved, it was far more sensual than seeing her body in the flesh. Her curves made silhouettes, and I found myself wanting to reach out and touch them — run my hands over every inch of them. When she bent over, I almost lost it.

I had to look away. I was excited, and there was nothing I could do about it.

"Don't be a peeping tom." I turned on the radio, trying to focus on anything other than a slippery wet Lilly in the shower — the water ricocheting off her body, travelling down her breasts, and making its way to her center.

"Jesus." I turned off the radio. I was becoming unhinged. I could normally control my feelings, but something about Lilly made me want to do things that I wouldn't usually think about, and that scared me. I was unravelling, and Lilly held the end of the string.

I stepped out of her motel room and into the hot summer sun. Sweat beaded down my body as I waited, but I didn't care. I'd needed to escape from this place.

After a few minutes of me trying to think of anything else besides Lilly's naked body, she met me outside.

"Everything okay?" she asked.

"Yep. All's fine. Just needed some fresh air."

"Okay." She nudged me playfully with her elbow.

It seemed out of character for her but helped me to lighten up. I was a man. I was a man physically attracted to this woman. A type of woman I rarely ever came across. That was what this was. Nothing more.

"I should be the one asking if you're okay." I searched her face for any indication of what was going through her mind. It had been a tough day, and Lilly seemed to hold all her emotions close to her chest.

"For now, I'm okay." She gave me a sad smile. "I have to be."

I wanted to ask her why she had to be okay. She had lost her parents—she was entitled to grieve. Instead, I walked in silence with her to my truck. I wondered why she wouldn't give herself one second to process the loss of her parents.

The drive to the morgue was awkward. I didn't try to fill the silence and neither did she. It was for the best, though. I knew the more I found out about her, the harder this attraction would be for me to resist. My desire for her would only become stronger.

"Sheriff, I've been waiting for you." Dr. Hicks eyeballed Lilly as he rushed us into the morgue.

To say it was a morgue was a big stretch. Usually a morgue was in the basement of a hospital, or in bigger towns, there was sometimes an entire facility. In Kittrell, though, the morgue was a part of the local doctor's house. Rather unconventional, but we didn't have many murders around here where bodies needed preserving.

"Typically, I'd let the other doctor handle this," Dr. Hicks stated as he looked at Lilly. "But the Sheriff here called in a favor and asked me to keep the bodies together."

Lilly walked in silence but gave him a small nod.

Dr. Hicks continued talking, and I held my breath waiting for Lilly's reply. "That's not the way we do things here. The woman would have been handed over—"

Lilly stopped dead in her tracks and turned to Dr. Hicks. "I'm sorry that my parents' murder made you go against your rules." Lilly's voice was soft, but there was an edge to it that made me shut my mouth and let her say her piece. "Despite the fact that my mother was black, she was a person whose life was taken from her in the most brutal of ways. So I suggest you point the Sheriff and me in the direction of their bodies and leave me alone to grieve for my parents." She was breathing heavily, a tear making its way down her reddened cheek, but she found the nerve to carry on. "While my mother was just another black woman, and my father just another white man who was corrupted by her wicked ways, they were my parents. They loved me and cared for me, and I will not let some pretentious doctor who is too ignorant to see the error in his thinking degrade their memory."

There was so much running through my mind. Should I have stopped her from talking? Everything Lilly said, though, was true. And truth was, I didn't want to control her. Not one single bit. My fear was that I wasn't sure how Doctor Hicks would respond. I was surprised when he opened the door to the identification room for her.

Dr. Hicks looked to me for some guidance. I softly shrugged. What was I going to say to Lilly? Don't speak the truth?

"You have five minutes," Dr. Hicks mumbled as he stormed away.

Lilly didn't glance at me as she entered. Two bodies were laying on the metal table. I followed her and let the doors close quietly on their own. I wanted to be there for her, but I also knew I needed to give her space. Again I was faced with the conflict of what the hell to do in her presence. She seemed determined to be okay because she had to be. I understood what she meant now. Watching the way Dr. Hicks had acted around her had made her statement clearer. She couldn't let her guard down at all. Anywhere.

I stood far enough behind her to give her space, but close enough that she knew I was there. I looked at the two bodies. They were covered from the neck down, and I was astonished at how much Lilly favored her mother with her heart-shaped feminine face and high cheek bones. She resembled her father too — the distinguished chin.

Lilly reached out and touched her mother's cheek then smoothed back her hair before she moved over to her father. She didn't touch him, she just stared. Then as if all her emotions overcame her, she crumbled in a heap on top of his body and pulled him close. I couldn't stand back anymore. I rushed towards her, then brought her against my chest.

She cried for a while. I wouldn't have called it weeping, because even in her grief, she was silent. Her tears seeped through my shirt. She needed to let this out — to release the grief.

Like Lilly had done to her mother, I smoothed back her hair as she cried until there were no more tears. There were small quakes of her chest as she struggled to find the air to breathe, to deal with her loss.

She looked up at me, her eyes still wet and puffy. "I'm not okay," she whispered as she struggled to breath.

I wanted to kiss her lips and breath air into her lungs. To stop her body from rejecting the emotion that she so badly needed to work through.

"It's okay to not be okay," I hoped she would listen to my words and give herself some time to grieve.

"Don't tell anyone." She brushed away tears from her eyes.

"Your secret's safe with me." I wasn't looking at Lilly anymore, I was staring at her lips. I didn't mean to narrow in on them, their fullness, how perfect they were while pouting. I simply couldn't hide what I felt in that moment. It was a time for secrets, and my secret was that I found Lilly irresistible, and the pitter-patter of my heart when she was around was more than physical attraction.

She didn't pull away at first, but when she eventually did, I felt her reluctance. Time wasn't on our side. She straightened out her dress, then took a paper towel and cleaned her face.

Dr. Hicks came back in, had Lilly sign some paperwork, and informed her that the bodies needed to be out as soon as possible for burial. Lilly agreed to make arrangements, and then we left. There was no talk about her crying, no talk of anything really in the car.

I couldn't resist, though. As we drove in complete silence, I reached out and squeezed her hand. She wasn't okay. I knew that now. She felt everything, much deeper than she let on. I didn't want her to carry that burden alone, and if I had my way, I'd be the one to help her through this.

Chapter Twelve: Lilly

"I appreciate you coming with me, Christopher. You didn't have to." I held the door handle ready to exit the truck. The engine was still running, the low humming sound vibrating underneath me. Or maybe I was the one who was vibrating from the close proximity of Christopher to my body. He leaned over me, then opened the glove box, taking out a gun. Checking the chamber, he stuck the gun in his holster at his side. But something had happened between Christopher and me.

At the morgue, he'd held me, and glanced at my lips like he needed them. Guilt swarmed me, as I had wanted him to kiss me when I'd been standing steps from my parent's bodies. I had pulled away when I so badly wanted to lean towards his mouth and let myself have that one moment.

Then in the car, when he'd squeezed my hand, I didn't want to let go. I held on tight — much tighter than I needed to — because holding his hand made me feel grounded, made me feel connected to something other than my clouded emotions.

"It was my pleasure, Lilly." He looked around outside and cut the engine.

"Go check on David and Matthew for me. I'm going to do a once over to make sure nothing's out of the ordinary, and I'll meet you in the office, okay?" He hopped out of the truck and stood there with the door open.

I liked watching him work, the determination in his eyes when he was protecting someone. I shuddered when I realized that someone was me. I doubted anyone would try anything with the sheriff around, but it seemed everyone here did whatever the hell they wanted.

"Okay." I opened the car, jumped out then walked into the office. I glanced behind me as Christopher nodded to me and went to review the area.

"David?"

The table had been set for when we returned. Three glasses and a pitcher of sweet tea. Heavy condensation dripped down the pitcher, leaving a puddle on the table. David wasn't there. Fear clawed at my chest when David or Matthew didn't round the corner. I walked to the back of the office, my unease increasing with each step that I took. I thought of all the possible scenarios. Maybe David had fallen. Oh God. I quickened my steps, the floorboards creaking underneath me.

I entered a large room searching each surface for any indication of where David and Matthew could be. My gaze immediately went down to the floor, and my heart jumped into my throat.

David.

His face was blue, his eyes large and bulging. I bit back a scream. He'd been beaten to death. My eyes took in the length of his body. Blood coated his face. Glancing up at the wall, I saw the words *Nigger Lover* covering the surface.

I averted my eyes when I saw those words. Words that made the reasons for his death painstakingly clear.

Because of me.

David had been able to survive an attack once, but this time, he hadn't had his youth behind him. Tears filled my eyes at the brutality of his death, at how innocent and fragile a man he'd been. It wasn't right, any of it.

On a bed next to the small amenity kitchen lay Matthew.

He was beaten almost beyond recognition, his body riddled with large gashes. The tears fell now, clouding my vision.

The sight before me was hard to stomach, but something propelled me to David and Matthew. I knew they were dead. Just by looking at them, there was no way anyone could have survived what had happened to them. But I had to be sure. I touched Matthew's skin, blood coating my hand. I put my fingers to his neck to see if he had a pulse. Nothing.

"No, David! No!" I wrapped my arms around his body, noting how stiff he felt. He had been murdered like my parents had, for what was right, for what he believed in. It was wrong.

I don't remember how I'd ended up outside, but I had. Matthew's blood was caked onto my dress and my hands. It dripped as my hands hung limply by my side, a trail of blood left behind me as I walked. I didn't care how crazy I must look, I had to find Christopher. We had to get David and Matthew out of there.

"Lilly?"

I heard his voice, but I couldn't see him. All I saw was David, his lifeless body, and the words written on the wall that were clearly a message meant for me to see. I saw them. I'd never be able to un-see them. It would be something I carried with me forever.

"Damnit. Lilly answer me."

My teeth chattered and my shoulders were being shaken. I was wandering, trying to find a place where any of this made sense. I blinked, and Christopher came into focus.

"It's David," I whispered, my voice hoarse and unrecognizable. Who was I? Was I weak? Unable to process this hate? "They killed him and Matthew, Christopher. They beat them to death." I held out my shaking hands for him to see.

Christopher's eyes widened as he spoke into his walkie-talkie and guided me to my room.

"It's okay, Lilly. I've got you. Nothing will happen to you. I promise." Christopher held me against as chest as I shook.

I didn't know what I was shaking for. Fear? No, it wasn't fear. It was anger, an anger now embedded so deep I didn't know how I'd come back from it. I dared any of those cowards to come after me.

Christopher released me, and I grabbed onto his shirt.

"Don't go," I pleaded with him. I wanted him close. Right now, that was what I needed.

A frown found its way to his face. "I have to help clean up the mess, Lilly, and find out what happened. Scarlett's here. Remember Scarlett?"

Scarlett appeared next to Christopher and put her hand on his shoulder. It wasn't a friendly touch, it held something more. The way she caressed it and let it linger. I didn't know what their history was, and right now that shouldn't have mattered. Thoughts of them together crept into my mind briefly, before David's grin replaced those dark thoughts that had no place in the moment.

"I'm going to help you undress and shower. Okay, Lilly?" Scarlett's voice was soft and comforting, and I nodded. Christopher released me, but kept our hands touching until the very last minute. Until he was gone.

"We'll need the clothes for evidence, okay?" Christopher said softly.

Scarlett hummed, like David did, as I undressed then showered off the blood. I didn't need her to bathe me. I wasn't that far gone. But not being alone was comforting. I couldn't make sense in my mind of what I had seen, of the reasons why they had harmed an old man who could barely walk. Their actions made no sense. None of these murders did. Of course, they never did.

I had the bathroom door ajar and heard Scarlett as she opened the door to my motel room.

"Thanks, Scarlett," Christopher said as I toweled off my hair then made my way closer to the bedroom.

Scarlett opened her arms for a hug, and my breath hitched in my throat.

Don't hug her.

Christopher patted her shoulder.

"Yes. Thanks, Scarlett. I appreciate it," I added, happy that he didn't hug her.

"Anytime, Lilly. I'm always here if you need me." She gave Christopher a quick glance. "Either of you. For anything."

Christopher cleared his throat and saw her to her car before coming back. She liked him. That much was obvious. I had hoped maybe she was here for me. A friend. My attraction to Christopher was based off two days of knowing him. Scarlett told me that she had been here her entire life. She knew Christopher better than me. They made sense. We most certainly did not.

"I need you to pack up, Lilly."

I finished pinning up my hair before giving Christopher my attention.

"For what?" Where could I go besides my grandfather's house? I wasn't ready to be alone. Even though staying at the motel meant I could feel David's presence everywhere, and it hurt, I'd rather be here than go to where my parents had been before their deaths.

"You're coming home with me. I'm deeming this motel a crime scene, and I wouldn't let you stay here even if it wasn't one. It isn't safe."

I put down my brush and focused on his words. Going home with him was just asking for more violence, not to mention the growing attraction I felt towards him. I turned to him.

"Christopher, wherever I am, it isn't safe."

Christopher moved so fast that, before I could blink, he was standing right in front of me. Our toes touched, and I held my breath.

"Lilly, it's my job to protect you."

I looked into his eyes and could tell he was serious. "Your job is to find out who murdered my parents. And now David and Matthew. I'm pretty much here asking for violence to find me." I sighed, turning away from him.

Christopher grabbed my arm, pulling me back towards him. My chest pulsed against his. The feeling, the tingles that traveled through me, brought me to life. My chest heaved as Christopher perused my body like I was the most important thing in the world. A wet strand of hair broke free and cascaded into my face.

Touch me.

Christopher reached up and tucked it behind my ear. Instinctively, I leaned my cheek into his hand, wanting him as close to me as possible.

"No, you aren't causing trouble. You're bringing to light the problems that have always plagued this godforsaken town." He moved his hand away from my cheek then took my hands in his.

He was almost pleading with me, which I didn't understand. Me going home with him would cause more trouble than I was sure I was worth. I liked it, though. I liked the look in his eyes that seemed desperate. His pupils dilated, and the beauty of his dark brown eyes even more visible. I liked when his skin was against mine, and the goosebumps that formed on my skin when he was near me.

"Come home with me, Lilly. Let me protect you and keep you close. Let me help you find justice for your parents, and for David and Matthew."

I didn't know why I trusted this man I barely knew, but I did. And right now, he was all I had.

"Okay, Christopher. I'll come home with you."

He smiled and let my hands fall to my side. I should have held him at bay, so I could have him against me for a few minutes longer. Truth was, I liked when he touched me. And that truth would most certainly lead to nothing but trouble.

CHAPTER THIRTEEN: CHRISTOPHER

1937

As Lilly packed, I questioned some other customers who said they saw a young man at the motel around the time of the murder. One said he was a black man, another said he was a white male wearing jeans, a T-shirt and boots. Yet another said a woman. I wanted to go with the description of the white male that was given by a bystander who claimed they saw someone fleeing the scene. The boot-prints alone fit the outline found at the crime scene for Lilly's parents.

But it wasn't enough. Not with the discrepancies in description. I was no closer to any leads than I had been two days earlier. I was thankful my father didn't show up throwing his weight around.

After Lilly had packed and I was done at the crime scene, we headed out to my house. It wasn't a long drive, which usually was great after a long day at work, but today was different. I tried to remain calm and positive about the case, but truth was, I wasn't. I needed to know who had murdered Lilly's parents, and she deserved that closure.

What made me even more uneasy was that the murderer was someone I'd most likely looked at every day for the past twenty-six years of my life. It was probably someone who David had known since they were kids, because there didn't seem to be much of a struggle. Not that David was any physical shape to fight back, and his grandson was never a fighter by any means. Regardless of how long this person knew

David, or the murderer's standing in our community, whoever it was had shown no remorse — they'd had no second
thoughts about beating them both.

I cringed at the memory of David's beaten body in the motel, where he'd spent his life welcoming others. It wasn't a
sight I'd ever want to see again. I'd known David since I was
born, and him having to die like that, for what? Because he'd
believed in something that this world wasn't ready for yet?

Matthew had been different from David. He'd believed in
the hate, or at least thought he did, as he had tried to follow
whoever would take an interest in him. Someone had probably seen him entering the motel and talking to me. He hadn't
told me anything. Fear had stopped him from turning in whoever had been behind the scare the night before. That fear
didn't matter anymore, because whoever it was had found
him and killed him. I had promised I would protect him and
David, and I hadn't. I'd fallen short on my promise. What
kind of Sheriff was I if I couldn't keep my own people safe?

I could fight crime, put people behind bars, or at least I had
thought I could. I'd never really had a big case, or anything
that remotely put me in harm's way. My instincts were sound,
and something in me knew that this case wasn't going to end
well. No matter which angle I looked at this situation, even
bringing Lilly to my home, they would find her. They would
make someone pay, especially if they knew how she made me
feel. They'd make us pay for that too.

Here in Kittrell, folk were set in their ways. It was all separate but equal — whatever the hell that was supposed to mean.
All I knew was that when I'd become Sheriff, I was told that
any calls to the black neighborhood weren't a priority. It
didn't matter what was going on. My own father had taught
me that.

Since the Porter's murder a few days ago, everyone spoke
in hushed tones, but the whispers all said the same thing —

Iris and Charles Porter deserved every bruise, every whip, every shot that was inflicted on them, and I was stupid to pursue it as a case. I couldn't live with myself if I didn't try to seek justice. Everyone deserved at least that.

"Well, this is it." I pulled into my long gravel driveway. The large plantation style home stretched across the perfectly manicured lawn.

"It's gorgeous," Lilly commented as she exited the car and taking in the scenery outside. "I guess my grandfather's house is probably like this, huh?"

"It is. It's beautiful. Even bigger than my house. We can go there. Whenever you're ready."

Lilly nodded, continuing to walk towards the steps.

"How do you keep up with all this property? And cleaning all those rooms!" She smiled as we walked side by side, the sun reflecting off her face as she quickly turned to me. After all that had happened, she was still able to find her smile. The sun highlighted the grace of her features.

"I have, um . . ." I hesitated. What do I call them? " . . . workers." She stopped at the door, and I skirted around her to open it.

"Workers?" She frowned. "You mean slaves." She put her hands on her hips.

"Lilly, don't be silly. There aren't slaves anymore. They work for me. They get paid, just like your mother did." My voice was wavering. Not because I was lying, but I knew no matter what I said, Lilly wouldn't be pleased with my response. I hadn't thought about how she'd react to hearing about Virginia and Jeremiah.

"Are they paid fairly?" She adjusted her dress and looked me. Her nostrils flared in anger as she tried to keep herself composed.

"Fairly, yes." I nodded. "When I took over the house, I changed a lot of things. Some opt to live here. Most though have families and homes. They can quit at any time. They get paid for the work they do. It isn't any different than how things are in the fancy town of Philadelphia, I'm sure." I may have turned an eye to certain things my father asked me to do, but this house was mine, and I ran it how I saw fit. Unfair wages and poor work conditions had no part of that.

"I'm sorry." Her face flushed. "I'm overreacting,"

I took a breath.

I knew Tucker had been a pompous ass towards her when they met the other day. He and my father were similar in a lot of ways, both willing to get what they wanted at any cost. Slept with anyone who showed them any attention and were complete and utter racists. I guessed it was natural for her to assume that I'd be the same. It bothered me, because I tried really hard to make it known that I didn't share the same sentiments as my relations. All without trying to make my father angry, of course, or bringing unwanted attention to myself.

"Let's go inside. It's getting warm out here," I said, trying to change the subject.

"Okay."

When I opened the door, the normally serene atmosphere was replaced with what could only be described as mass chaos. Virginia ran around, brooms and dust pans flying.

"Christopher Alexander Weatherby!"

I stopped dead in my tracks, and Lilly bumped into me.

"Next time you decide to have a house guest, give me more than an hour's notice. You have no idea how much time and effort goes into — oh!" Virginia ended her tirade as Lilly came from behind me.

Lilly smiled and extended her hand, but Virginia bypassed it all together and brought her in for a hug.

"Well, my word." Virginia let Lilly go and took her face in her hands.

I thought I caught the glimpse of tears rimming her eyes.

"You're easy on the eyes, aren't you?" She studied Lilly's face, the way one does when sensing a familiarity. I hadn't told Virginia who I was bringing home. Lilly resembled her mother. That was probably what she was seeing. Iris in her daughter.

"Thank you, ma'am. It's a pleasure to meet you. I'm Lillian Porter."

Virginia quickly glanced to me, her smile temporarily replaced with pursed lips. I knew I wouldn't hear the end of this. Bringing Lilly here, into my home, would bring unwanted headaches, but I knew she wouldn't be safe anywhere else. Not after what had happened to David and Matthew. The murderer had proved that they were willing to go to whatever means necessary to make their point. Apparently, killing Lilly's parents wasn't enough.

"I'm Virginia Perry. Housekeeper here at the Weatherby estate." She let Lilly go and stepped aside. "I'll show you to your room, so you can rest and freshen up." Virginia's demeanor had changed. She'd gone from being captivated by Lilly to wide eyed and alarmed.

"I'll do it."

The deep voice caused Lilly to jump.

"Sorry, didn't mean to scare you. I'm Jeremiah." Jeremiah extended his hand.

"Nice to meet you, Jeremiah." Lilly shook his hand. She gathered her bags and began to walk towards the stairs.

"Ma'am, I can get those for you." Jeremiah ran towards Lilly.

"Jeremiah," Lilly said sympathetically as she stopped and looked at him. "You don't need to help me, serve me, or do anything of the sort while I am here. I am perfectly capable of carrying my own bags, of cooking my own food, and of running my own bath." She stiffened and adjusted her bags. "I just held a dead man in my arms because he took care of me and I don't want you to end up the same."

Jeremiah and Virginia glanced at each other quickly. Lilly's mood had shifted, and I was now on full alert. She didn't want anyone helping her. I understood it. After what she'd seen, I could only imagine what was going through her head.

"What have you done, Christopher?" As tears filled Virginia's eyes, I knew this was more than superficial concern.

"What's wrong?" I rushed towards her. I wasn't used to this side of Virginia. She was always in control, and I'd never seen her cry.

"How could you bring her here, after all that's happened?" Virginia brushed the tears that kept falling from her face.

"I'm the Sheriff. I have to find out who murdered her parents. She wasn't safe at the motel. It's my job."

Virginia wiped her eyes with the sleeve of her dress. "There's more to this than you realize, son." Virginia put her hand on my shoulder. "I just hope you're ready for what you are going to uncover." And with that, she walked away.

I was left with my thoughts and now my increased worries. What did Virginia know that I didn't?

Chapter Fourteen: Lilly

1937

I didn't like how I was feeling. It had been but a few days since my parents' murder and I felt strangled, frustrated. A fervor so fierce it threatened my resolve to find my parents' murderer. My feelings were a mix of emotions that didn't go well together. Not ever, and especially not now.

I had come here to bury my parents, to find out what happened to them, and to move on with my life. The death of other people who were supporting me was not supposed to be in the cards. And Christopher Weatherby had definitely not been in the plan.

He was different than other men I'd met. His genuine concern for his town showed his caring side, and the way he opened doors for me, respected me in front of his brother, who would have rather seen me thrown out to the wolves without a second thought. He wasn't like his brother. He was kind. He treated the people who worked for him well, but I couldn't help but think I was a hypocrite for being attracted to someone who had paid servants still in his home. What was he allowing? He was giving them a job, wages, and a roof over their head.

God, I am confused.

I was blinded by the pain that my parents had endured and seeing things in Christopher that didn't exist. He was a good man. Yet I still found myself questioning the what ifs. I always had my head on straight, could see through any problem and knew there was a solution. The way Christopher was making me feel, I didn't know if there was a solution that was acceptable for these times.

My thoughts went back to David and Matthew. David had been a truly good, simple man who was taken from this earth in the most brutal of ways. I couldn't help but think, had I not been here, had I not kissed his cheek, or he kissed mine, would any of it had happened? There were so many questions, and at the end of it all I was the common denominator.

"When you're done unpacking, if you like, I can show you around town. Take you a few places."

Christopher was standing in the doorway to my room. Propped up against the door frame, he rubbed his face and his hands together a few times. I smiled knowing that my presence confused him just as much as his confused me. I should have said no. I should have tethered the emotions and ended the confused state of my mind. Too much had happened over the past week. I was sure I'd crack at any moment.

"I thought it might be good to get our minds off things for a bit. Kittrell isn't all bad. We have some good things."

Good things. Like David. Like you.

"That'd be great. Thanks." I opened my bag and started pulling out the clothing I'd brought with me. So much for my resolve. "Let me put these things away and change." I didn't look at Christopher again. I wanted to, but I had to try to keep myself under control. I had seen what happened to David when he got close to me after one day. Christopher cleared his throat, and I kept my eyes focused on the task of hanging my dresses.

"You are beautiful just how you are."

Hearing his footsteps move away, I fought the urge to watch him go. Those thoughts of Christopher had now manifested themselves into something more tangible. A sensation, like tiny goosebumps, traveled throughout my body. Even after he'd left, those words kissed my skin, traveled down my neck, my back, and stopped right in the pit of my stomach before melting into feelings of attraction.

I tried to hurry and unpack, dying to be close to him again. To hear his words that, while they weren't necessarily poetry, seemed to affect me deeply. I might have hated my attraction to him, but I couldn't stop those feelings. I could fight them. I probably should have tried, but they felt good when I was broken. Everything about Christopher healed me.

I met Christopher downstairs and we headed out. As we drove in his truck and passed the motel, I averted my eyes, not wanting to see the place where everything had transpired that morning. I wanted to shake off the guilt and the pain of what had happened. But those emotions were there, a permanent fixture in my chest, like my heartbeat, beating and fluttering. I could feel the strength of that guilt and pain in the loss of my parents. Now my heart held the loss of David and Matthew as well.

"This is the town center. And over down that street would be the Mayor's house." He pointed out the window to a small patch of grass where there was a water fountain. Small businesses lined the street, people milling about and waving to the Sheriff. That was, until they realized who was sitting next to him. Scowls found me as he kept pointing and talking about his town with pride. His town, I kept reminding myself. He lived here, worked here, supported, and protected these people. He had no reason to fear them, when I had every reason to. Anyone of them might have killed my parents without a second thought.

He pulled into a parking spot on the small street then came around to open my door.

"This place has the best ice cream." He shoved his hands in his pockets. "Do you like ice cream?" He shook his head before I could answer. "I should have asked. Please tell me you like ice cream?"

I smiled at his nervousness.

"I love ice cream." *This isn't a good idea.*

We shouldn't have been out after what happened to David and Matthew. Our presence was adding more ammunition to the fire. My mother's voice came into my mind, reminding me that I didn't have to hide. That by doing so, it meant you were guilty, and I was guilty of nothing other than wanting to live my life like any other person. I stepped out onto the street then followed him as he started walking towards the door to the ice cream parlor.

It's just ice cream. I can manage that.

"Great. I hope you don't mind me stopping. I'm sure you want to get right to planning the funeral. I just thought maybe it'd be a good thing." He paused, standing stiff.

On instinct, I moved closer to him and placed my hand on his shoulder.

"It's fine. Thank you. Ice cream makes everything better."

He exhaled, and his body relaxed. Christopher turned towards the door of the ice cream parlor then stopped. He removed his hands from his pockets and balled them in fists at this side.

I opened my mouth to say something, but before I could, Christopher grabbed my elbow and pulled me away, rushing me back to the truck.

"What's going on?" I looked around us, my senses on alert.

"Nothing. We're leaving." He opened the truck door, practically shoving me in before slamming it shut.

He slid into the driver's side then cranked the engine. A small vein on the side of his neck was bulging.

What the hell is going on?

"Christopher!" I said his name sternly.

He turned and faced me.

"What happened? You can't just drag me away from the ice cream parlor after asking me if it was okay if we stopped." I gripped his knee. "What happened?" I asked softly.

He placed his hand over mine and sighed. "They won't serve you here." He shook his head in disgust. "I'm an idiot."

"How are you an idiot?" I questioned, removing my hand from his knee.

"I never looked." He cut his gaze to mine. "I've never had to look. It never mattered to me."

It all clicked now. He had never taken someone like me with him. He'd never needed to know who could and couldn't be served at restaurants. He never had to be aware of signs that were plastered on all the business in the town center. Any business reserved the right to deny service to me. Not just me. All of us. That was my life. Constantly looking to see if I could walk into a store without being shooed away. Checking to see if I could drink from a water fountain without foul language and words of contamination and disease being yelled at me. And in Christopher's world, there was none of that. Just ice cream whenever he wanted, and fountains at his disposal.

I didn't respond to him. I couldn't, because I wasn't sure what would come out of my mouth. I took the anger that boiled inside me and I balled it up. I was going to use it. I was tired of being angry and saying someday things would change. Now was as good as time as any.

I exited the truck quickly and with a resolve that propelled me forward. Christopher screamed my name—right as I made my way to the ice cream parlor, I saw him running after me from the reflection in the window. He wasn't fast enough. I was fueled by anger and I was going to do something about it. I was going to make a stand.

I opened the door, and all heads turned to me. A couple sat at a table in the corner holding hands, and I smiled at them. The girl stared at me, but it was almost as if she had seen a ghost. She looked to her boyfriend. He immediately stood and went over to the counter as I sat at a table and scanned a menu. I didn't want ice cream anymore. I had lost my appetite. It was the principal. I had a right to be served.

The young couple rushed towards the exit — the girl being dragged behind him. She gave me a small smile. Like me not being able to sit down and order ice cream was nothing. Fact was, to many people, it was nothing. I didn't belong here. I wasn't welcome. The sign made that clear.

Well, screw that sign.

"Lilly." Christopher held the door for the couple to exit before fully coming in.

"Sheriff, I'm glad you're here. This woman waltzed in and sat down." The man who was behind the counter pointed at me. "Apparently she missed the sign."

I put the menu on the table and looked up at the two men in front of me. I didn't know what this man was capable of. And this guy — I squinted to see his name tag, Jeff — was about to refuse me service. The question was, what was Christopher going to do about it?

"I saw the signs." I motioned to the door where the sign hung. And the wall. And the counter. *No blacks served* was plastered everywhere. Talk about overkill. "I chose to ignore them."

Jeff folded his arms across his chest. "That's not how it works here, lady. I can refuse service to anyone I want."

I smiled. "You can. That is certainly your right. You didn't refuse service to the couple that just left." I removed a one-dollar bill from my pocket. "My money is the same color as theirs." I placed it on the table.

"But your skin color isn't."

Christopher inhaled sharply.

I saw red. Never had I ever been so blatantly disrespected in my life. Christopher grabbed my elbow again. I didn't like his hands on me. Not when he was trying to stop me. I ripped my arm away and stomped over to the ice cream freezers. I leaned over, took a cup then scooped myself two helpings of vanilla. The irony wasn't lost on me that my favorite flavor was vanilla.

"Lilly!" Christopher marched over to me, and Jeff ran behind the counter, his face beet-red.

"Sheriff, arrest her!" he demanded, slamming his fists on a table.

I took out more money than needed and threw it at him. "Keep the change." I went to walk away then stopped at the door. Christopher whispered to Jeff. I'm sure he was trying to calm down the situation I had caused. Screw that. Those signs, this separate but equal crap, were never going to lead to change when people skirted around the real issues. If people let places hang those signs and deny service, all because of the color of someone's skin, the things that had happened to my parents would continue.

I headed back over to Christopher, then took his hand in mine. It gave me the strength to continue and to finish what I'd started. Christopher furrowed his brow as he looked down at our intertwined hands. Then his eyes softened when I caressed the top of his hand with my thumb. Christopher glanced back up at Jeff, who looked at us with his mouth hanging open, speechless at my actions, and how Christopher was letting this happen.

Suddenly, his hand in mine wasn't enough. I needed more. I wanted more. Leaning in, I kissed Christopher on the cheek. That kiss was for David, for Matthew, for my parents, but more importantly that kiss was for me. God, was that kiss for me.

"Vanilla's my favorite." I released my hand from Christopher's and then licked the spoon. While it wasn't a smart idea to taunt and egg Christopher on, I wanted him to do something other than skirt around the issues that were staring us right in the face.

I was angry and wanted him to know that no one—I didn't care how hot you were, or how you made my body ache to be closer to yours—would hide me. No one would deny me the simple pleasures in life, like freaking ice cream, because they were too afraid to stand up for what was right. I knew I'd made it crystal clear, because the fire that burned in Christopher's eyes made me squirm under his gaze.

I hated that he was even more attractive when he was angry. That was something I was going to have to get a handle on. I had bigger stuff to deal with, and unless Christopher stood up for what he believed in, rallied behind me fully, he was not worthy of my time.

CHAPTER FIFTEEN: LILLY

1937

"Don't you ever put me in that position again!" Christopher gripped the steering wheel.

We were parked outside his house, and I was staring out the window, trying to focus on something other than being scolded by Christopher.

"What position? To do something that's right?" I glared at him. "You're a hypocrite. You tell me you want to do the right thing, but when the time comes, you run away."

"It's not as simple as taking ice cream."

I gritted my teeth. Granted, it wasn't my finest moment, but I had to start somewhere.

"I can't protect you from everyone, Lilly." He released the steering wheel. "There are certain people here that aren't as open-minded as some."

I started to respond.

"Don't." He shook his head. "There's a large chapter here that support keeping everything separate. Which I'm sure you're aware of, after what happened to David and Matthew. They catch wind of what you pulled tonight, and they will be marching on my doorstep threatening to drag you out!" He flung up his arms.

"What do you care? You don't know me. You don't have to protect me. And you took me out for ice cream instead of chasing down the murderers' trail and shoving them all in jail to rot." I let out a small laugh. "Then you rush me out of there, instead of sticking up for me."

That was what was funny. The way he couldn't decide what he wanted. He wanted to protect me and seek justice. Yet, when he had the opportunity, he hadn't done anything about it.

Christopher slammed his fist on the steering wheel. "I thought that it would be a nice distraction. Branson, my deputy, is trying to get some leads on who could be involved, but nothing as of yet. I'm trying here, Lilly. These are all people I know." There was a small crack in his voice. "These are people who I grew up around. It isn't easy. It's not a switch that can be flipped, and all of what they've been taught since before they could walk magically disappears."

I sighed. I understood what he was saying. I was expecting a lot, especially from someone I'd just met.

"Do you think it was easy for me to hear my parents were murdered and to identity their bodies? Do you think it was easy to find David and Matthew like I did?" I brushed the tears that had fallen down my cheeks. I couldn't do this. I had to get away. I had to remain focused. "You know what? I'll get my stuff and stay somewhere else." I went to open the door, but he reached out and grabbed my hand. I shivered when his skin brushed mine. His skin was hot with his anger, but the heat soothed me; the heat and brought me a sense of calm that I hadn't had in a while.

"I care, Lilly, or I wouldn't have told you that the ice cream parlor didn't serve your kind here, nor would I have asked you to stay at my house." He took a breath–as if to hesitate. "I wanted to protect you from that. I know things are a little different in Philadelphia. That you aren't used to the way things are here."

"I know. I appreciate that. But in order to change things, we need action. Not words. You're the Sheriff. You hold power." I opened the door and then stepped out. "David said that. He said he saw great things in you."

Christopher's shoulders slumped.

"I don't have any power here. I saved you from going to jail just now, sure." He shrugged. "But my father controls this town. Nothing will change while he's running things. So, I keep my mouth shut and my head low. That's all I can do."

I held the door handle to the truck in my hands. It was solid, and it kept me grounded. I needed that, because with each word that Christopher said, it was like he was drifting further and further away from doing what was right.

"That's all you think you can do. If you want change, you have to take chances. Like me coming down here. That was a chance. I probably have no job. I have no family anymore." My voice cracked. "But I got on that train and came here. Because I believe in this so much that it doesn't matter what happens to me. I had to try to make it right. Whatever the cost."

He studied me for a moment as he digested my words. "I know. You're right. It takes a lot to change things, though. It's much more than stealing ice cream." He smiled, and I couldn't help but join him.

Taking that ice cream hadn't been the best idea. It was just ice cream, though. I wasn't asking to go to a white school or asking to marry a white man. I looked at Christopher as I shut the car door prior to heading into his house. He fell into step behind me.

Sometimes what was simple, plain, and generic really wasn't. Christopher looked to be clean cut, an average man, a vanilla man. It'd only been a few days, and already I was unravelling some of the complexities that I knew were buried inside him. His controlling father, his own struggles with what was right and wrong. There was hidden pleasure beneath that exterior. The sparkle in his eye when I'd taken his hand in mine, the low growl I'd heard coming from his throat when I pressed my lips to his cleanly shaven cheek. Vanilla wasn't simple at all. The flavor held much more promise than I had ever given it credit for, and it was most definitely my favorite.

Chapter Sixteen: Christopher

1937

I watched her walk away, keeping my distance to give her space.

God, what have I gotten myself into?

When she had stomped out of the truck and walked into that ice cream parlor, I had thought I was going to be sick. My badge would only get me so far. Especially once my father caught wind of what was going on. And after David and Matthew, I knew violence was already on the table. They were a warning. Lilly didn't give a damn about that warning. She was torn up about David and Matthew, yes, but her mission was bigger than any one person. Her determination was bigger than her, or me, or this town.

Lilly's beliefs ran deep. Watching her lean over and scoop out that ice cream had made me want to ravish her mouth with mine and tell her that I'd protect her, always. I wasn't sure I could keep that promise. The need to protect her was the only reason why she was staying at my house tonight.

Although I kept questioning my pull towards her, as we had met yesterday, we weren't complete strangers .The truth is that knowing someone wasn't etched in time — truly knowing a person was carved in the degree to which there was trust and comfort. Lilly trusted me. And even though she shivered when I touched her, and her breath hitched in her throat whenever I got close, the actions weren't discomfort. I knew deep down they were a yearning far more complex than anything I had known could exist.

Instead of following Lily inside, I headed around to the back of the house. Jeremiah was bent over a flower bed, sweat pouring down his face.

"Hot one, huh?"

Jeremiah stood and brushed sweat away from this brow. "You try pulling up all these damn weeds." He yanked hard at one, and it barely moved.

I rolled up my sleeves and started pulling with him. We worked for about two hours, not saying a word, just yanking, swearing, and getting dirty. It was therapeutic after what had happened with Lilly. I was able to get rid of some of my pent-up anger.

"You going to tell me why Lilly came stomping into the house earlier?" Jeremiah asked out of breath. He didn't even look at me, he just kept pulling weeds.

"Humph" I scoffed.

"That bad, huh?" he asked.

"She went into the ice cream parlor in the center of town. I tried to take her in there and didn't realize they wouldn't serve—" I coughed trying to figure out how to phrase what I wanted to say without sounding like an asshole. Frankly, there was no way around it. "Her kind," I added.

Jeremiah stiffened. "Our kind?" He looked at me pointedly.

What is it with everyone today?

"Yes, your kind," I corrected myself. "I've never looked. I've never had to look. I tried to hide it and take her home without her finding out, and she stormed in there and took ice cream."

Jeremiah inhaled sharply. "Took ice cream?"

"Yes. She bent over the counter and scooped out some vanilla ice cream."

I took off my shirt and wiped my face with it. It was hotter than hell, but now that the sun was starting to go down, the intense heat was going with it.

Jeremiah shook his head and smirked. "I must admit that the visual of her leaning over the counter and taking ice cream is funny. And the look that must have been on Jeff's face." He let a smile flit across his face before he turned serious again. "She's going to get herself into trouble here. I'm not sure about her."

I raised my eyebrows. "What about her? She's here because of her parents. What more is there to know?"

"I know that. I was here when you were told what happened to them, and now, with David and Matthew . . . She isn't from around here. She doesn't know how things work." He snatched up his flask from the ground. "Yet she storms down here like she's going to fix everything. She won't be able to. She's going to make things worse." He took long gulping sips of his water.

"Jeremiah." There was an edgy tone to my voice. A warning to not talk about Lilly in any negative way.

"You like her. I can see it. That's why you're angry."

I looked away from him. *Damn, am I that transparent?*

"You arrest her?" Jeremiah asked as he folded his arms across his chest.

"Of course not." I studied the ground.

"Exactly. If it was anyone else who had done what she did today, you would have hauled them off." He took another gulp of water. "You have a soft spot for her, and it's going to be trouble for us all." Jeremiah walked back up towards the house.

Maybe he was right. I was too clouded by her pretty face to make a sound judgement. Being with Lilly, helping her, was going to bring a lot of unwanted attention and backlash on us all.

CHAPTER SEVENTEEN: LILLY

1937

I helped Virginia prepare dinner as best as I could. I wasn't the greatest cook. My mother wasn't either, so I hadn't had a solid teacher. Virginia tried her best to guide me through the process, but when I accidently got eggshells in the bread mixture, she shooed me away.

"Just like your mother, you sweet thing." Virginia patted my hand.

I wanted to ask her about my mother, pick her brain about her childhood and her love affair with my father. It seemed their life really started when they moved to Philadelphia. Something had always nagged at me though. Like I was missing something, an entire piece of my parents' past. They would speak in hushed tones, but when I entered a room, they stopped. Sometimes, I'd catch my mother silently weeping.

"Sorry." I grinned as I washed off my hands then set the table. Jeremiah came storming in only to stomp up the stairs without saying hello.

"These boys . . . Worse than females," Virginia said as Christopher walked in, the door slamming behind him.

"Christopher," I blurted out.

He turned towards me covered in dirt. He was shirtless, his toned stomach glistening with sweat.

"Can we talk?"

Virginia looked at me from the corner of her eye as she focused on kneading the dough.

"Not now, Lilly. I can't." He too stomped up the stairs, and the slamming of his bedroom door made me jump.

"Christopher was fickle, even as a boy. He knows how to a hold a grudge."

I slumped down in the kitchen chair.

"Don't take it personal. It was probably something Jeremiah said." Virginia patted my shoulder. "Those two are always fighting like brothers."

As if things could get any worse, Tucker walked in.

"What's she doing here?" Tucker stood in the doorway, his eyes black and focused on me.

"Your brother offered her a place to stay after what happened at the motel." Virginia explained.

I wrung my hands in my lap, unsure of what to say. Tucker seemed like a ticking time bomb, and I feared what he'd do if I even said hello.

"That bitch has no right to be here. She's been nothing but trouble since she came to town."

Tucker wasn't a kind man, but he was right. I'd got David and Matthew killed. Was I worth the trouble? How many people had to die before I had answers?

"Language! She's our guest, and if you can't respect that, you can go stay with your father."

I breathed in sharply at Virginia's tone. I glanced between the two of them wondering if Tucker would say anything else to her. Instead, he turned on his heels.

"I'll get my things, then." He looked back just as he was ascending the stairs. "Who knew my brother would turn out to be such a sympathizer?"

When he was finally out of sight, I buried my face in my hands.

"Child, don't let him bother you. He doesn't know better." Virginia slipped a cup of tea in front of me and patted my hand. "All he knows is hate and violence. Christopher lucked out when he decided to go his own way. He always had a softer side." Virginia took a sip of her tea. "Tucker is a lost soul, and the bigotry gives him a purpose."

"It's hard to believe that he and Christopher are brothers," I commented.

"I know. They are like night and day."

Silence passed between us. There was so much more I wanted to know. Virginia seemed to know everything about everyone. Yet there was a sadness that engulfed her. I could only hope that in time she'd trust me enough to share what happened to her. What made her live out the rest of her life working for Christopher when she had other options? I was left wondering what Virginia had to live for.

CHAPTER EIGHTEEN: CHRISTOPHER

1937

The creaking of the floorboards woke me up from a sound sleep. As I opened my eyes, I saw Tucker looming over me.

"You brought her here . . . to our home?" Tucker ripped me out of bed, and I hit the floor with a thud. I didn't need this. Not now.

"This is my house and I can do what I damn well please." I brushed myself off then stood, ready for whatever Tucker had up his sleeve.

"You need to think long and hard about what you're doing, brother. You're tarnishing the Weatherby name each time you show that fucking poor excuse for a woman kindness."

I sat down on my bed and stared up at my brother. My baby brother. When had he become so far gone and invested in the poor treatment of others? Where had I been?

"I've failed you," I said quietly.

Tucker stopped pacing and focused on me.

"What?"

"I didn't help you and guide you onto the right path in life. I let you roam around and hoped for the best. Now look at you." I shook my head. "You can't even see Lilly as a person." I glanced down as he clenched his fists at his sides. "Are you going to hit me? Your own brother?"

"I don't know who you are anymore. You're everything I've fought to not become. You love Lilly. A black woman."

I opened my mouth to protest, but he stormed away mumbling about how he was leaving.

I lay back in my bed replaying the past couple days in my mind. A lot had changed. My life had turned upside down since Lilly had come walking into it. I couldn't blame her, though. She had a higher purpose that was bigger than me or Tucker. He'd give up on this hate, one way or another. I couldn't help but feel that Lilly was right. In order to make a change, you needed action. Not just words. And I was ready for whatever would be thrown my way.

The next day came quickly. I wanted to go to Lilly, to apologize for yesterday and for brushing her off, but some distance was for the best. It would give us space to clear our heads. I opted to head into work to get a head start on things.

"Running out before she wakes up?" Jeremiah sat outside on the porch.

"No," I mumbled.

"Don't be a coward, Christopher. Don't stop fighting for what you believe now." Jeremiah's gaze found mine. "Not now, when it matters, to all of us."

I spun my keys around in my hand as I slid into my truck and drove away. I wanted to be different and stand up for what I believed in. My beliefs were all mine. They went against everything I'd been taught, everything my father had tried to embed in Tucker and me. Those beliefs didn't scare me anymore—I was ready to accept who I was. I was a man willing to do whatever it took for the right thing.

CHAPTER NINETEEN: LILLY

1937

The day went by slowly. I woke up and intentionally passed by Christopher's room only to find that he had already left for work. I helped Virginia in the kitchen again, trying to take my mind off thoughts of Christopher. Despite our exchange yesterday, he mattered to me—in whatever way meeting someone just a couple days before could matter to a person—and that terrified me.

Dusk had finally settled in when I decided to focus on the logistics for my parent's funeral.

"Dinner will be ready momentarily." Christopher stood in the doorway to my room.

I was elbow deep in paperwork and procedures when his voice swam through me. It was like butterflies, fluttering in my stomach and making their way throughout my entire body. Goosebumps, warmth, all of it made me want to reach out to him. I turned from the desk, and I couldn't help but stare. He had replaced his uniform with a pair of jeans and a T-shirt. He looked comfortable, relaxed, and at home.

Home.

Where was my home now? I still lived with my parents back in Philadelphia, but the thought of going back there, without them, seemed impossible.

"Great," I said in reply to his announcement. "Thanks, but I'm not really hungry. I'm trying to figure things out." I turned back to the paperwork. I didn't even know where I was going to bury them. Money wasn't ever an issue for me, but when I had asked the cost to transport their bodies back to Philadelphia, I nearly choked.

"Figure what things out?" Christopher moved closer. He motioned to the chair. "Mind if I sit?"

"No, of course not." As he walked past me, the scent of him surrounded me. It wasn't any of that fancy cologne, no. Christopher smelled like soap and aftershave. I breathed in, willing the scent into my mind and cataloguing it as a permanent memory.

"So." He crossed his legs. "What are you trying to figure out? Can I help?"

Everything that had happened yesterday seemed to be water under the bridge. I wasn't sure how I felt about pretending the incident at the ice cream parlor hadn't happened. I didn't know what else we had to hash out, but something had shifted within Christopher. He was calmer, more relaxed, and I decided to go with it.

"Just my parents' funeral. I guess I'll have to bury them here." I shuffled through some of the papers. "Looks like we have a family plot at my grandfather's house. That's the most logical place."

Christopher grit his teeth at my mention of burying them together. I know it was unheard of, to bury races together, but it was my property now. I could do what I wanted. There was nothing the law could do to stop that.

"Is that a problem? I'm the only living Porter, the house and land become mine, correct?" I hadn't meant to sound confrontational, but I certainly didn't want to have to fight about where to bury my parents.

"It is your property and within your right." Christopher rubbed his face. "I'm afraid how people will perceive things once they catch wind of what's going on."

I dropped my pen and stood. "I honestly don't care. If you

didn't notice yesterday, I don't take kindly to being told what to do. I think it's safe to say people know I'm here and what I stand for." I loomed over him. "My parents are dead, Christopher. Murdered by someone in this town, and I will not separate them in death when they would not separate themselves in life. They fought for what they believed in and their right to stay together. I will uphold that." I stood tall. Christopher stayed in the chair and smiled at me. I was shocked at his reaction. I'd expected him to do what he'd done at the ice cream parlor — try to talk me out of it, to tell me no, something. But I hadn't expected a smile.

"All right, then. Let me know what I can do to help."

I breathed a sigh of relief.

He isn't fighting me. He wants to help.

He shifted in the chair, and I glanced down. My body heated when I saw the outline of the effect I was having on him pressed against his pants. I was overheated and I resisted the urge to run my finger across the outline. If he only knew the effect he was having on me, too.

"I don't have anyone here." I took a deep breath. "I actually don't have anyone at all. Do you think you could be there with me? For the funeral?"

Christopher looked down at the floor. I shouldn't have asked. I didn't want him to feel obligated to do anything more for me than he already had.

"It's okay." I bit the inside of my cheek as doubt filled my mind. "I shouldn't have asked that. Especially when it might cause problems." I turned on my heels to walk away. "I'm going to go to dinner."

Christopher stood quickly and grabbed my hand. He was talking to me, but I didn't hear anything. All I could focus on was the warm sensation that started at my fingertips and moved all the way up my spine. I was slowly coming undone, and I couldn't control it any longer. I shivered and snatched my hand out of his.

"Stop. Let me help you," he said.

I held my hand close to my body, the sensation still pulsating under my skin. I was captivated and enthralled by this man who stood in front of me, and by the impact he was having on me. I wanted to experience that sensation again, feel it in my toes, across my chest, wherever I could.

"Okay," I whispered.

Christopher seemed content at that response and headed down for dinner. I promised that I would be right behind, but took the opportunity to watch him descend the stairs, the pull slowly melting away. Movement from the corner of my eye caught me off guard. I jumped. I glanced down the hall and saw Jeremiah staring at me. I waved and smiled but all he did was turn and go, leaving me tense.

I'd caught him staring at me a lot, studying everything I did. While it should have made me nervous, it didn't. He seemed serious, with his furrowed brows and pursed lips, but something about his demeanor let me know he was harmless. I knew I had to be careful, but like my mother, I could read people. And Jeremiah didn't seem like a threat.

When I went down to dinner, I took a moment to appreciate the beauty of Christopher's home. The tall ceilings, the wooden floors that creaked when I walked across them. Lining the walls were portraits of people I assumed were Christopher's family all smiling down at me. I stopped in front of a portrait of a woman who favored Christopher. Her long dark hair framed her body that was hidden beneath her dress. She was distant—her eyes not quite focused on anything.

"That's Christopher's mother."

I gasped at Jeremiah's voice.

"She was sick. After having Christopher, she went mad."

I turned to him, but he was gone as quick as he came.

Taking one last glance at the portrait, I ran my fingers across the painted canvas.

"I'm sorry you were misunderstood," I whispered. I too felt mad. I composed my thoughts and made my way down to the dining room.

I chose my spot across the table from Christopher. It was a large table, one of those fancy ones that were meant for dinner parties. He was so far away, and we had virtually no conversation.

"Where are Jeremiah and Virginia?" I had to raise my voice for him to hear me. I knew Jeremiah was on his way to the kitchen, but I must have missed him.

"Right here, Suga'." Virginia came in with a tray of food and put it on the table. She moved over to Christopher, took his plate and started serving him.

My stomach growled but I ignored it. Had Virginia eaten? Why wasn't she enjoying this meal that she had worked tirelessly for?

"This isn't right," I said.

"What? I can't hear you. I'm sorry," Christopher said as he focused intently on his food. He remained unfazed by the situation and it infuriated me.

Virginia looked at me, her eyes widening and almost willing me to stay quiet. I couldn't. I wouldn't. Actions spoke louder than words.

I stood, grabbed my plate and went to the food Virginia had brought in. I made up the plate, all while they both stared at me.

"Sit," I said as I pulled out the chair for her.

Virginia shuffled from foot to foot. She seemed nervous. I guess having someone call out your boss would do that to a person.

"Lilly, listen to me, she's the cook," Christopher explained.

"She isn't a cook. A cook does just that — cooks. She's here serving you like you're a prince or something."

Christopher hesitated. I waited, hoping that he would say

something to make what was happening go away. He made no motion to change anything. He let out a loud sigh and leaned back in his chair.

"I can't . . ." I stepped back from the table putting my hands up in defeat. "I can't do this." I ran out of the dining room and up to my bedroom.

My stomach growled again, and I pushed my hunger aside. I laid my head back on the pillow, the darkness that had settled over the house casting shadows on the wall. I kept tossing and turning, thinking about what my life would be like now. My mother would never get to hold her grandchildren, my father wouldn't walk me down the aisle. The thoughts were selfish, I knew. They had been taken from this world long before their time. I turned over on my back, the sounds of chirping grasshoppers and howls out in the distance further enhancing my discomfort. I let the tears fall, sobs filling the silence. I finally fell asleep from pure exhaustion, the memories of my parents finding their way into my dreams.

"Rise and shine, darling."

I groaned, prying my eyes open and sitting up straight in the bed. "Morning, Virginia. What time is it?" I stretched, shielding my eyes as she opened the curtains.

"Nearly midday. Christopher said to let you sleep as long as you wanted, but you're going to sleep the day away!" She came and sat down on the edge of my bed.

I stiffened at the sound of Christopher's name.

"Give Christopher some time, dear. I know you want things to change, but they can't change overnight."

"I know. I felt I was betraying my mother by sitting there and letting you serve me."

"Child, your mother would have been ecstatic if she knew you were here with me and I was cooking you food. And

Christopher is like my son. I wasn't serving anyone, just doing what any mother would do" She smiled and puffed out her chest. "Your mother loved my cooking"—she paused—"and Christopher is a kind man. I doubt he has a cruel bone in his body. I raised him, yanno?" Pride beamed from Virginia.

I had gathered as much when she mentioned Christopher, Tucker, and Jeremiah in our conversation the other day, but hearing her say it made me smile.

"He told me to go live my life, but I chose to stay, to be by his side, and Jeremiah's. Those are my boys, and I hope someday I can see them get married and have children of their own." She patted my leg, tears glistening in her eyes.

I hung my head low because I was embarrassed by my actions last night. My outburst was simply a manifestation of my own issues that I was unfairly projecting on this household.

"What about Jeremiah?" I questioned. "He speaks to me briefly and then disappears so quickly. Why did he stay?"

She sighed. "He's been with me since he was a baby. I am the only momma he's known. Mr. Weatherby did a lot of awful things to him while he was growing up. I think he stayed because of me. He didn't want to leave me alone."

"He hates me. I know he does." I held myself close. "It's the way he looks at me."

"He doesn't know any better. People from a wealthier less hardened society rarely come around, and none of them have ever been kind. They treat us the same as Mr. Weatherby did. Like we are trash and have no feelings or purpose other than to be there for their every whim. You're different, though." She smiled and placed her hand on my leg.

"How so?" I questioned.

"I saw it in your eyes. That look. Determination. I can spot it anywhere," she mumbled.

The topic was getting too heavy for me, and after the previous evening, I was drained. "Thanks for waking me up. I didn't sleep well last night." I got up from the bed, shuffling through my unpacked bag for an outfit to wear.

"Stay. Talk with me. I've been known to be a good listener. At least your momma said so."

"My momma..." My interest piqued, I dropped my clothes and sat back on the bed next to Virginia. "You knew her well?"

"Yes, I knew her. I knew her better than anyone."

I glanced at Virginia. Her words held much more meaning, but before I could ask, she continued to talk.

"She was bright and beautiful. And stubborn as an ox."

I grinned. "My dad always said that about her. He said I got that from her."

"He loved Iris. Loved her more than he ever loved anyone."

All I could do was nod and smile. I knew my father and mother had a love unlike any other, but hearing it from someone else touched me deeply than I imagined. I grew up watching them, enamored by how well they meshed. I had never thought about that for myself until now. Until Christopher.

"Tell me everything, Virginia." I took her hands in mine. "Tell me everything you know about them." More tears flowed, from both of us now. The heaviness of this conversation didn't bother me anymore. I was with a woman who knew my parents when it had all happened—who knew of their love affair. I wanted to know every detail, both good and bad.

"In time, child. In time." She gave me a quick hug before pulling away and taking my face in her hands. "Promise me you'll never doubt your parents love for each other, or for you. Regardless what you find out. Okay?"

"Okay," I croaked, wondering what she meant "Where's

Christopher? I want to go see my grandfather's house and finish planning their funeral." I gathered my clothes.

"He had some business to take care of. Jeremiah can take you wherever you need to go."

I bit the side of my mouth. I thought of the few times he had spoken to me and the curtness that lingered underneath the edge of his voice that made me unsettled. Jeremiah wasn't a bad man, although he certainly was trying to make me think he was. I saw right through him.

"Don't be nervous. He's harmless. He's lived a hard life. We could use some smiling around here."

Virginia was right. I could help Jeremiah, be his friend, and show him a different life, how things ought to be.

"Okay, I trust you." I opened the door to my bedroom. "I'm going to take a bath and then I'll be ready to go." I walked down the hall to the bathroom, feeling slightly better. Virginia brought me a comfort every time she was around me.

"Please, Lord, keep her safe," I heard Virginia say as she walked past the bathroom.

I'd never seen the violence before, but I'd known it was there, hidden behind faces and masked as normalcy. In just a few days, I had been subjected to attacks and verbal abuse. It didn't matter, though. I was ready for answers, and answers were what I intended to get.

Chapter Twenty: Christopher

1937

"How's it going, boss?" Scarlett smiled as she entered my office holding a steaming cup of coffee.

I took a sip, the first taste hitting my tongue. I moaned. I'd got zero sleep last night. I had heard Lilly's soft cries and I'd fought back the urge to go to her, hold her, and tell her how stupid I'd been. Like the coward I was, I stayed in my bed, staring into the dark, listening to her crying. I understood her conflict with how dinner had been served. I'd just wanted something nice for her, a dinner where we could sit and enjoy each other's company.

"That good, huh?" Scarlett grinned.

Scarlett was a beautiful woman. I'd never deny that. I didn't think she cared much about me, other than the fact that I was her boss. She wanted a husband with a good standing in our town. A Weatherby? That'd be a catch. Hence why I was pretty sure she had been sleeping with my father.

"It's delicious, thank you. I needed it." I returned to the pile of paperwork on my desk. I didn't want to be here. I wanted to be at home with Lilly, helping her handle the burial of her parents.

I glanced up as Scarlett lingered in the doorway. "Did you need something else?" I put the paper down and gave her my full attention. I didn't want to be rude.

She shut the door then glided towards me. Her hips were seductive as they swayed back and forth as she continued to move in my direction. I had always been able to distance myself from Scarlett's intentions, but lately because of Lilly walking into my life and causing sexuality to pulse through me, I was struggling to contain it. She came around my chair and slid her hands over my shoulders, squeezing them tightly then massaging out all the tension I hadn't even known had built up there.

"That any better?"

I let out a small sigh. It was good. Virginia always told me that I carried the weight of everything on my shoulders.

"Lilly," I breathed out.

Scarlett pressed her lips against mine. I didn't kiss her back. I pushed her away, and the bile crept in my throat at the thought of being with anyone else. No one could compare to Lilly, not even a woman as beautiful as Scarlett. She stepped back even further and stared at me.

"It's her, isn't it?" Scarlett straightened out her dress. "That's why you won't kiss me? Lilly's why you don't want me?"

"There is never going to be an us, Scarlett." I rubbed my face. I'd messed up. I shouldn't have let her touch me. "I'm sorry if you thought I could give you more. I can't." I sighed.

"I just thought that we were pretty much made for each other. You'll be mayor one day I'm sure, and I'm—" She smiled and moved her hands over her body. "Well, I'm a good catch. I'd be a good wife to you."

The hurt and the tears in her eyes pained me to see. "You're a beautiful woman, Scarlett, and you'll make a man a good wife someday, but that man—it isn't me."

She scoffed and turned towards the door.

I didn't want this turning into a big deal, nor did I want rumors filling the office. Scarlett, like any other person, wanted attraction, passion, love. She thought she could find that in me, but I was spoken for. Whether Lilly knew it or not.

"You're great at your job, Scarlett. I don't see any reason why this has to be odd between us. We can go back to the way things were."

She spun around on her heels and glared at me. "Don't worry, Sheriff. Your secret's safe with me." Scarlett winked before returning to the main office.

I shook my head and picked up the phone to check on Lilly. Scarlett wouldn't be any trouble. She'd move on to the next man who caught her eye, or to my father.

"Hello," Virginia answered.

"It's me. Just checking in."

"Christopher, she isn't here. She's going off to her grandfather's house with Jeremiah."

I growled.

"Don't growl at me, boy," Virginia scolded.

I recoiled. I may have been a grown man, but Virginia knew how to discipline me.

"Sorry," I mumbled.

"She wants to bury her parents together."

I supported her decision. I wanted to be with her whenever these pivotal moments were taking place. To protect her, but to also show her that I supported her decisions.

"She knows it's against the law, but she's a lawyer, and said she can do what she wants on her property. All that land is now hers. No disputing that," Virginia said confidently.

People were already talking about what had happened at the motel and the ice cream parlor, and they were asking questions. I had fielded more visits and phone calls about Lillian Porter and what she was doing here this morning. It was just a matter of time before something else happened.

"I'm going over there." I hung up the phone, grabbed my badge and gun, and rushed out the office. I swung open the door and almost ran into Scarlett. She blushed before moving out of my way. I didn't have time to worry about her broken heart or whatever was going on with her. I'd made myself clear. I wasn't interested. My focus was on Lilly, on helping her, whatever the cost and that cost was getting more and more expensive as each day went on.

Chapter Twenty-one: Lilly

1937

"Are you ready, Ma'am?" Jeremiah stood at the doorway to my room, his head hung low.

"It's Lilly, not Ma'am," I said with a smile.

"Uhuh," Jeremiah mumbled and stepped aside as I walked past.

"Where to first?" I asked as we descended the stairs.

"I thought maybe we could go to the house first." Jeremiah once again wouldn't make eye contact with me. "Virginia said you would be burying your parents there and you wanted to check it out first."

I hated this—the struggle I was sure he felt about how to act at times. I wanted him to be comfortable around me.

"Jeremiah." I stopped once we reached the front door then placed my hands on his shoulders. He went rigid under my touch. "Look at me."

He slowly brought his face up to meet mine. I hadn't really looked at him earlier when we first met. I'd been too consumed with everything that was going on. He was handsome, strikingly so, with skin similar to my caramel complexion. He was a little taller than me, and his deep-set hazel eyes held much more than I was expecting to see. Pain. Loss. Struggle. I saw it there, and I wanted nothing more than to bring him close and let him know I'd never let anyone hurt him again. But I didn't know him, so I settled for my words.

"I want you to know that I am not like the people who

wronged you in the past."

His eyes became slits as he scrutinized my words.

"I'm like you and I want . . ."

Jeremiah snickered. "You aren't like me, Ma'am. You come from a world much different than mine." He pulled away from me. "Have you ever been beaten for breaking something by accident?"

I added to the distance between us, my hand instinctively going to my neck.

"Have you ever had scalding water thrown on you for not working hard enough?" He pulled up his shirt, exposing his puckered and scarred flesh. I gulped. He shook his head as he brought his shirt back down. "I thought not. So, next time you want to try to reach out to me, comfort me, just don't. We are nothing alike, and you have no idea what I've been through."

He opened the door and held it as I walked out. That certainly hadn't gone as I had planned. I'd wanted him to understand that while I lived a different life, not privy to the physical hardships that many had endured, I had been subjected to discrimination, but not the same as Jeremiah. I guess that did make us different.

We drove in silence to my grandfather's house. I had never met the man, and from what I gathered, he wasn't the caring, compassionate type. He'd pushed my father, accepting only the very best out of him, which was great and had made him a wonderful man and a fantastic lawyer. The problem was, the picture-perfect life my grandfather had had in his mind did not have my mother in it.

When we pulled up, the vast driveway looked like it went on for miles. The house took up a lot of space — there was nothing around it, only land. No people, no cars. It was eerily peaceful. Pillars held up the porch, drawing the eye to the front door. The white paint chipped. More in a lived-in way that said someone had loved this home.

I smiled as I ran my hands down the front door. I wondered when my father was a boy if he had run around these open grounds playing hide and seek.

Taking one last glance out at the open land, I acknowledged what had happened here before my parents' time. Hardship. Abuse. It left a sour taste in my mouth, and me more apprehensive about entering. Jeremiah walked in silence to the door, opening it with a key that I assumed Christopher had given him. I didn't ask. It seemed best not to say anything after what had transpired between us earlier.

I stepped into the entryway, the hardwood floors and spiral staircase laid out in front of me. While the beauty of the home captivated me, the smell brought tears to my eyes. This house smelled like my mother. Like freshly picked flowers, roses to be exact. Subtle, yet refreshing. Tears rimmed my eyes as I walked up the staircase, and I let my hand linger on the shiny banister. I followed the smell, hoping that maybe it would lead me to her. I silently and foolishly wished that when I turned the corner, she'd be there, smiling at me. She'd pull me into a hug, ask me about my day, all while father laughed and teased me as he often had.

But they weren't there. I was alone. So incredibly alone.

I opened the door to a bedroom. My parent's suitcases and clothes were strewn about. I leaned over, picking up their clothes, piece by piece. I did it without thinking, trying to distance myself from remembering why I was here in this house. The sun reflected off something, blinding me. I followed the reflection and found myself at a table at the end of the room. There, placed together, were my parent's wedding bands. They had never taken them off. Seeing the rings there, like that, hit me. They'd known. My parents had somehow known what was coming for them.

A sob wracked my body as I clutched the rings in my hand, my fingers going numb with the pressure of my grip. I felt dizzy as though I was going to pass out, but then two strong arms wrapped around my body.

"Shh. It's going to be okay."

Jeremiah.

"Why are you here?" I croaked out. "You made it clear that we are nothing alike."

"Because this is one thing we both have in common. We both lost our parents."

I studied his face as he stood in front of me and I allowed him to hold me. It wasn't romantic, it was an embrace shared by two people who had lost their parents. No more words were spoken, we just sat on the bed, staring out the window, lost in our own memories.

CHAPTER TWENTY-TWO: CHRISTOPHER

1937

I drove faster to the Porter's house than I had ever driven. I wanted to be there for her. To make sure no one tried anything while she laid her parents to rest.

When I arrived at Lilly's grandfather's house, I wasn't alone. "What's with everyone trying to get in my way today?" I hopped out of the car, and my father walked towards me.

"Son," he said.

"Father." I tried to muster as much respect as I could, but I knew he wasn't here to check on me. He wanted to figure out what was going on.

"I'm here because I received a disturbing call regarding the burial of Charles and Iris." He cleared his throat. "As well as a story about Lillian Porter entering an ice cream parlor. A whites' only ice cream parlor."

I crossed my arms. News sure did travel fast.

"They won't be buried together. It's against the law," he advised.

The demand in his words angered me. My father had done a lot of things I disagreed with over the years, but I had sat idly back while he'd done them and never spoke up for what was right. Lilly, and the murder of her parents, had made me aware of this on numerous occasions over the past couple days. She was right. I had to make a stand. I looked at my father who waited impatiently for me to respond to him.

Forget it, there is a first time for everything.

"She's burying them here."

His eyes widened. "Excuse me? You're the Sheriff. Arrest her!" he yelled.

I glanced at the house as Lilly's face appeared at the window. Jeremiah pulled her back.

"Or have you forgotten your duty? You obviously didn't arrest her yesterday when she stole ice cream."

"No, I didn't arrest her. I handled the situation with the shop owner, and he opted not to press charges. This is her property now, and although it is the law that races cannot be buried together, the law does not mention anything regarding private land. It only involves public burials."

Damn I'm good.

"You're making a huge mistake, son." He clenched his fists at his side. "You'll be sorry. You'll regret protecting her."

"The only mistake and regret I have is not speaking up sooner. This is wrong. All of it. While I never supported it, I didn't do anything when you told me to turn a blind eye or I pretended to not see some injustice because that was what was expected of me." My breaths were shallow, and my words were hard to find, but I had to get this out. Not for Lilly, for me. I needed to show my father that I was a man now with my own thoughts and beliefs which I intended to follow. No longer would I walk in his shadow. "I'm the Sheriff and will uphold the law for every citizen. White or Black." I walked away without a glance at my father. I was sure he was in shock at my blatant disregard for his order. I knew this would come back to haunt me, but right now, I didn't care.

Lilly opened the door right as my father drove off, and she ran right into my arms. She wrapped her arms around my neck, and my hands instinctively went around her waist. I pulled her close, so our bodies were flush against each other. She fit perfectly against me, as if her body were made for me.

"Did you mean it? What you said?"

I held her a second longer before setting her away from me,

so I could see her face. "I meant it all. You have a right to bury your parents on your property." I brushed past her and glanced at Jeremiah brooding in the corner of the room.

I knew she wanted me to say that I thought it was all wrong, that we should be able to love who we wanted, marry who we wanted, and I did. But I also knew my father would hold true to his promise, and that I would regret what I said. Not because I'd said it. What I had said was the truth. But I'd regret the hurt it would bring on those I cared about. I just hoped it wouldn't mean any harm would come to Lilly.

CHAPTER TWENTY-THREE: LILLY

1937

I did what I could in a day. I needed to bury my parents and offer them the peace in death that they didn't have in their last days. I was thankful that Christopher had stood up to his father, and his actions meant more to me than he knew. But the way he brushed me off afterwards, and the distance he had been putting between us over the course of the past day stung.

I gathered flowers and headed to the plot I had picked out on their land. I'd chosen a spot under a large oak tree, separated from the rest of the family plots. None of those people buried there had cared about my parents or how deep their love ran.

I stood in front of their graves. I'd had someone make two simple gravestones, displaying their names. Each stone had been carved with a simple saying, *A love more than skin deep.*

I was alone. No one had come. I didn't expect anyone would. Who cared about my parent's burial in this town? Absolutely no one. The day was quiet and hot, the sun hiding and partially masked by the big tree I stood under. I had never minded being an only child—I'd liked the individual attention my parents gave me. But here, now, burying them and struggling with their loss, a sibling to share in the grief would have made it all easier to manage.

"Can I join you?"

My body reacted to the voice with a tingle. The numbness

I had felt, standing here by myself, went away. I turned around to find not only Christopher, but Virginia and Jeremiah were walking close behind him as well. I nodded, fearful that if I spoke, I wouldn't be able to hold the tears at bay.

Christopher, Jeremiah, Virginia, and I stood there in silence. No one said anything but they were there for me, and I didn't feel as alone. I heard sniffling next to me, and I looked over at Jeremiah who held Virginia in his arms. She wept, tears streaming down her dark face. The way Virginia cried was heartfelt, from the depths of her very soul. I could only imagine what it was like to know they died such a horrible death.

I went to her, to offer her comfort, but also to allow myself the chance to let my emotions free. Because once I was in her arms, I let it go, all of it. We cried together, for two people who were taken brutally from this world. I didn't sob, they were silent tears, but they took over my body, my shoulders shaking under the pressure of the feelings that had been unleashed.

"Come on, suga. Let's go inside, I brought some food over with me. I'll make some dinner."

Dusk had finally settled in by the time we left the oak tree. Christopher and Jeremiah had taken off to get some things from Christopher's house. We all decided we'd stay at the old Porter plantation that night, so they could help me go through things in the home.

"Virginia?" I sat down at the table as she hummed, whisking something in a bowl.

"Yes, dear?"

"Are Jeremiah and Christopher close?" I drew my fingers over the lines on the table. "They seem much closer than Tucker and Christopher."

Virginia wiped her hands on her apron and turned to me.

"Jeremiah and Christopher are only a few years apart.

They were raised in the same house, and both are stubborn." Virginia smiled. "Fredrick, Christopher's father, was a mean man, even when he was younger. He took out all his anger on poor Jeremiah."

"I don't want to know." I shook my head. It was too painful to think of a poor child abused.

Virginia continued whisking. "Lilly, I believe that you're here for the right reasons. But there is a lot more to the injustices that you are fighting for. Jeremiah was scalded with hot water if he brought coffee too hot to Fredrick. He was made to sleep outside if he forgot the simplest things." Virginia wiped her eyes with her apron.

I stood up from the chair then went to the window as I dissected what Virginia had said. Jeremiah and Christopher were walking towards the house, Jeremiah laughing as Christopher stumbled and almost fell to the ground.

"Why him? Why did Fredrick target him?"

Virginia began to answer but the door opened and Christopher and Jeremiah burst through, joking and shoving each other.

Christopher's gaze met mine, and Jeremiah looked at me, too. There was a hesitation I saw in his eyes, but then it gave way to a small smile. Jeremiah placed a kiss to Virginia's cheek.

Jeremiah nudged Christopher, and they both came either side of me and placed kisses on my cheeks.

"For the ladies of the house," Christopher said. "Don't wipe my kisses off!" Christopher playfully brought his hand to his chest.

"If you knew how to kiss, I wouldn't have to!" I wiped the side of my face again. "Slobbery." I was joking, but something in the air changed. Jeremiah cleared his throat and mumbled something before leaving the room. Christopher stared at me with such intensity.

"I know how to kiss, Lilly." He leaned in close to my ear. "I can show you."

Virginia slapped him with the dish rag, and he shot me a grin before following Jeremiah. I was left completely flustered and utterly confused. He'd gone from virtually ignoring me to offering to show me how to kiss.

I was thankful for a reprieve from my thoughts when Virginia asked me to the set the table. If she hadn't, I might have gone after Christopher and done something completely unladylike.

Virginia made another amazing meal, but this time we all sat together at the table. It felt like a family — a mismatched family. I smiled to myself glancing at everyone.

"This lemon meringue pie is to die for." I moaned softly as I let the fluffiness hit my mouth.

Christopher grunted, and I thought I spotted him adjusting himself underneath the table. Did this typically happen when a woman made noises? I wasn't well versed in sexuality, but I wasn't dense. I knew what happened to my body when I found a man attractive, and what was going on in my mind and body when Christopher around was even better.

"Wahoo. Let's get 'em." Loud voices carried from outside.

We all glanced at each other before jumping up and moving to the window. The headlights blinded us as a truck pulled up in front of my house.

"How'd they know to come here?" Virginia asked.

"My father," Christopher mumbled and cursed under his breath. "Stay here."

Christopher took his gun out of his side holster and cocked it. Jeremiah went behind the door and grabbed a baseball bat I hadn't even known was there. I stood staring intently out the window. I had never seen anything like it before. Even at David's motel, I hadn't seen the men. I'd just heard them, and that was enough to put fear in my soul.

Now I saw everything. About six men were in the truck, their faces covered with white masks, hiding behind them like the cowards they were. I'd have had more respect for them if they'd shown their faces. Let everyone see what the face of an ignorant bastard looked like.

As they piled out of the vehicle, I looked for their weapons. I didn't see any guns, and I thanked God for that. But there was rope, a chain, and a bat like Jeremiah's. We were severely outnumbered. Their six to our two.

No. We have a fighting chance if I stand beside them. I can help them. I can help Christopher and Jeremiah. United.

I straightened my dress, stormed towards the door then walked out to the porch with Jeremiah and Christopher.

"Get inside," Jeremiah hissed, trying to push me back.

"No. I won't let you guys do this alone. It's my fight, too." I squeezed Jeremiah's hand.

Christopher glared down at me, a sadness in his eyes as he looked at my hand in Jeremiah's. I couldn't focus on that now. I couldn't think about how I wanted to kiss him, about how I'd liked that he'd been clearly turned on at the dinner table tonight. I vowed if we made it through this, I'd pursue the pull I felt towards Christopher. Because who knew when my time on this earth would be up? I didn't want to die not knowing what his lips felt like against mine just because I was afraid.

The door to the house opened again, and Virginia came out and stood next to me. "Well, I can't just stand inside either."

I placed my other hand in hers, and we stood there, hand in hand waiting for whatever fate had come for us.

CHAPTER TWENTY-FOUR: CHRISTOPHER

1937

I knew this would happen. I was surprised they waited this long to show up.

Lilly touched Jeremiah again. It burned my eyes and a lump formed in my throat watching her reach out to him. I wanted her. I did. And as I stood there waiting for whatever was going to happen, I felt it even deeper. She was strong. In the face of all that was happening she hadn't left us to handle this ourselves. She wanted to be a part of it.

"Well, well. Look what we have here." They all piled out of the truck then moved towards the porch.

"Sheriff." One of them addressed me as I tipped my head in acknowledgement. He held a shovel that he bounced between his hands, the clacking sound vibrating throughout my body.

"We've just come to get her off the land."

Lilly stiffened next to me, and my heart rate quickened. They wouldn't touch her. Over my dead body would they lay a hand on my mother. I stepped in front of her to shield her.

"Not her." Another one snickered. His voice was familiar, but I couldn't quite place it because the mask he wore muffled his words.

"They shouldn't be buried on the same land. You know the laws here," he said.

"This is my land now and I can do what I please on my property, so please vacate the premises." Lilly moved forward as she spoke. I noticed her hands shaking, but her voice was strong, and she was so beautiful standing up for what she believed in.

They all laughed.

"You're beautiful." The intruder fixed the eye slits on his mask, and they opened wider. "That's all everyone keeps saying. Just like your momma was."

I rushed forward and put my hand on the small of Lilly's back. A loud whistle came from one of the men.

"Guess Sheriff here already claimed this one as his whore." He snickered. "Bet she's a good screw."

I clutched the gun at my side. "Take the mask off and say that to my face."

But he wagged his finger at me then walked away towards the oak tree.

They sang, a song I'd never heard before. It sent chills up my spine.

Nigger, Nigger, hanging from a tree.
Ain't no one coming for me.
I can kill, any of you I want.
'Cause you're nothing but an infestation.
Smash, Smash, under my shoe. Ain't no one, coming to save you.
Ain't no one coming to save you. Ain't no one coming to save you.

Lilly's breathing quickened as her body heaved against my touch. They were crazy. Each and every one of them.

"Stop!" Lilly screamed and rushed down the stairs. Her hair broke free from her bun, and she was sprinting past the men.

"Inside, Virginia," I yelled. She nodded, and the door slammed shut behind her.

"Jeremiah." I motioned for him to come with me as we ran after Lilly.

Damn. How is she so fast?

"I won't let you touch them. Stay away!" She threw herself

over the graves, her arms stretched as far as she could across them both.

"Move her, Christopher, before I have to kill her where her parents lie."

The mention of my name sent shivers down my body. Whoever was under that mask was someone I knew.

"Lilly, please," Jeremiah pleaded as he held his hand out to her.

She shook her head violently as the tears fell. "No. Kill me then. You have no right to do this." She stared at the men through her tears.

"We do, darling, because Sheriff here won't do a damn thing. Never has. Never will." He spit and it hit my shoe. He lunged forward and grabbed Lilly's arm.

Where I would have normally thought this through, I didn't now. I moved quickly and elbowed one of the men in the face, so I could get to her. Lilly was screaming and thrashing as she was ripped away from her parents. He threw her on the ground, and I was thankful that he didn't do anything worse.

Jeremiah was being held back by two men, trying with everything he had to stop what was going on. I leaned down, then lifted her into my arms. Feeling the rise and fall of her chest was a comforting sensation amidst the chaos. She was alive. She was safe.

"Enough!" I yelled, holding Lilly in my arms. She wept against me, her body shaking with each breath.

"You're nothing but a nigger lover." A hard swing of the shovel hit the gravestone, pieces shattering. Lilly jumped, and I held her closer, shielding her from what was happening. Swings, kicks, punches, everything that they could do, they did to that gravestone when in reality, they really wanted to do that to us. I sat back and watched, wondering how I was going to protect Lilly from what I knew was just the beginning.

Chapter Twenty-five: Lilly

1937

The masked men sped off in the truck after all the destruction they caused. I was thankful my parents were unharmed, but their gravestones were demolished. Mere crumbs of what used to stand.

Christopher still held me, and as he watched them speed away, he clutched me tighter against him.

"We should probably get to bed. It's late." Christopher focused upward, the moon reflecting off his face.

I shivered as he then stared at me, my body pulsing with desire. He was a complex man. He had offered to help me, protect me, yet he gave the impression that he was struggling with something.

"We can all just stay here at your grandfather's house. I wouldn't trust them to not come back."

It was true. Christopher clearly didn't want to leave me here alone as he kept reaching out to me whenever he could, and these men would stop at nothing to make a point. Truth was, it wouldn't matter where we stayed, they'd find us if they wanted to.

"Yeah," I said as he released me, and that comfort and safety I'd felt in his arms went with him. I wrapped my arms around myself, trying to get that feeling back, but the movement was useless. I wanted him.

"Oh, how awful." Virginia brought her hand to her mouth as she walked towards the graves that were now all rubble.

Jeremiah had begun picking up the pieces, laying them in neat piles. I didn't know why he was doing that. He did it intently with such focus that it made me smile. He was a gentle soul.

"Jeremiah, it's okay. I can do this." I placed my hand on his shoulder, and he looked up at me. He held a piece of the stone, and I saw that my mother's name was carved on it.

"I wanted to hurt them." His eyes were transfixed on the stone in his palm. He caressed it, running his thumb over the shattered piece.

"I did too," I whispered as I moved closer to him. He needed comfort. That feeling I had when I was with Christopher.

"No. You don't understand. I wanted to kill them."

"It's okay. Come on. Let's go inside." I glanced back at Christopher who stood watching Jeremiah and me — the fire in his eyes unsettling. He looked irritated, but I didn't care. Jeremiah needed me.

"Okay." Jeremiah shoved the piece of stone in his pocket and walked towards the house.

I went to follow Jeremiah, but Virginia's words stopped me.

"I've got to go clean the kitchen." Virginia mumbled as she continued picking up broken stone.

"We can do it tomorrow." I placed my hand on hers.

"I have to do something. It helps me forget."

I wanted to forget, too. But I wanted to forget everything in Christopher's arms. I kept telling myself that my choice to be with Christopher would bring trouble, but trouble was already here. What the hell did I have to lose?

I closed my eyes and sat on my bed, trying to free myself from the thoughts of Christopher's hands on my body, the closeness of him as he held me. But none of that seemed to matter.

"Lilly?" Jeremiah stood in the doorway to my bedroom looking beaten, broken, and fragile. His clothes were disheveled and his hair a tousled mess. He was soft and kind and hoped a better world like I did. He needed me now. I could give him that. I could take someone else's pain away. Maybe he could even take mine away.

"Stay with me, Jeremiah. Just for tonight. I don't want to be alone." The words escaped from my mouth before I lost my nerve, but I wouldn't take them back.

He didn't say anything. He just walked towards the chair then sat there as I wept. We both fell asleep, seeking solace in each other's company. Jeremiah's proximity brought on none of the sexual desires I had with Christopher. His nearness, however, did bring the comfort and protection both he and I sought for the night. I drifted into dreams of my parents in a world where there was no more hate—just love, acceptance, and peace.

Chapter Twenty-six: Christopher

1937

"Stop being a child and tell her how you feel!" Virginia was making biscuits, eggs, and bacon for breakfast. I sat at the table drinking coffee as she chastised me.

"I don't know what you mean." I took a sip of my coffee.

She turned towards me. "I'm not an idiot, Christopher. I see the way you two are around each other." She placed the biscuits in the oven. "So, tell her already."

"It's not that simple."

Virginia took a cup down from the cabinet and poured herself a cup of coffee then sat down next to me. "Don't talk to me about simple. Will it be easy? Absolutely not. Will it be worth it?" She raised her eyebrows. "That's up to you two. But it seems fate has intervened, and you two are made to be together, much like Iris and Charles were."

I rubbed my face. "Jeremiah." That's all I said. I'm not sure what I meant by that, but I'd noticed they were closer. Almost closer than Lilly and I were. I didn't want to steal his girl or come between a relationship that was blooming, especially when Jeremiah was like a brother to me.

"What they share is different. Trust me on that." Virginia patted my hand then continued to finish cooking.

I could agree with her on one thing. I needed to talk to Lilly. I hadn't been able to talk to her last night. Her fear hadn't been the only thing that had brought her into my arms. I knew there was something more between us.

I headed up to her bedroom to talk to her before I lost my nerve. My palms were sweaty against the bannister as I ascended the stairs.

Don't let your nerves get the best of you.

When I got to her room the door was wide open and Jeremiah was asleep on the chair next to her, and Lilly was asleep on the bed. He'd been there for her, when I was too much a coward to make sure she was okay.

I cleared my throat as I stared into the room where Iris and Charles had shared some of their last moments. I hadn't been sure that I could protect Lilly and be with her in the way I so desperately wanted to be. I'd needed to step back last night and examine my emotions. I'd thought my feelings were clouding my judgement, but now, everything was clear. She had to be mine.

"Christopher." Lilly turned towards me, a sad look stretching across her face.

"Are you okay?" I moved closer, eyeballing Jeremiah. He stared back, his eyes almost daring me to say something to him.

"I'm fine. Last night was hard, you know?"

"I can imagine. I hope Jeremiah here took good care of you."

She smiled, putting out her hand for Jeremiah to take then helping him up from the chair. I wanted to break his hand for touching her and being near her. They looked closer than two average people would be in just a night together. Maybe Jeremiah was what she needed. She was calmer, more at peace, and that was all I wanted—for her to not be suffering. That didn't stop the low growl from surfacing in my throat. I couldn't look at them together because all I thought about was how I should have been braver and come up here after her. How her hand should be in mine.

"I think we should hunt around, separate, go through some stuff, and pack up whatever isn't needed," I said, clearing my throat.

No, that is a lie. I want to talk to Lilly and get them apart.

"Didn't you come here already for anything that might help with the case?" Jeremiah questioned.

I didn't like his tone, at all. Suddenly he was acting protective of Lilly, when I knew days prior he'd been unhappy about her being here.

"She just buried her parents, and their graves were destroyed. Give her time to grieve!" He loomed in front of me, a time bomb waiting to explode as he clenched his fists at his sides.

"I know what happened. I was there." I ground my teeth together. "And yes, I was here. The day after it happened. I only looked in the general areas, quickly, before my father called me for a meeting. Another once over could prove useful."

Jeremiah grunted before storming out of the room.

"Sorry about him. He's temperamental." I apologized, moving into the bedroom then sitting on a chair.

"I know. It's okay. He's a good soul. I can feel it." She placed her hand over her heart. It was endearing really, the faith she put in others. She trusted Jeremiah, and she'd trusted me.

"You're trusting him pretty easily, huh?"

Lilly stopped in her tracks as she went to leave the room. "I suppose so. I'm usually not, but there is something about him that makes me feel comfortable." She shrugged.

I knew she meant it. Her kindness would only take her so far, especially in the world we lived in.

"I'm sorry about last night. I shouldn't have gotten involved, but my parents . . ." Tears filled Lilly's eyes. "I wanted to protect them. I wasn't here to protect them before."

I nodded.

"I've decided that I'm going to stay here and not go back to your house at all," she stated confidently.

"Lilly . . ." I groaned out her name. "That's not a good idea. After last night, it's the worst idea yet. They will come back."

"I know. That's why it doesn't matter. Someone is going to say or do something regardless of where I'm staying. I can't put any more people in danger." She took a deep breath. "And you being with me is fueling the fire. I won't risk your life for mine."

The softness with which she said those words showed that she cared. I knew she did. I looked at her. A fire burned within her, a determination that superseded anything.

Talk to her. Tell her how you feel.

"I don't like this." I said.

I'm nothing but a coward.

"Quite honestly, I'm not your concern. You met me what? A few days ago? I appreciate your hospitality, but I am staying here." She turned to march out of the room and ran right into Jeremiah.

"I'll be staying here with Lilly," Jeremiah said.

I clenched my jaw. My frustration threatening to bubble over. Most likely it would bubble over in the form of my fist against Jeremiah's face.

Lilly hesitated, glancing between Jeremiah and me.

"Let me help you." Jeremiah said with a concern I wasn't used to hearing.

She focused on him again before nodding. "That'd be great, Jeremiah. Thank you."

"Jeremiah will watch over me. Problem solved." Lilly smiled at me, as she and Jeremiah both walked out of the room.

"Jeremiah!" I yelled after him once Lilly was down the stairs. He paused then turned to face me.

"Yes?" Jeremiah said through his teeth.

"Why were you two in her room like that?" I pointed to the bed and chair like a child whose favorite toy had been taken away from him. I knew Jeremiah wouldn't hurt Lilly. I trusted

Jeremiah more that I trusted even my own brother. I didn't like their close proximity—the way he held her. The way she let him. Now he was going to be staying here with her. Alone. I had no claim on her. She made that very clear. But it didn't mean I couldn't make sure she was safe.

"Is everything okay with you. You are acting almost jealous?" Jeremiah said, quirking his eyebrow.

"No. I just . . ." I paused.

Who am I kidding?

I was jealous. "She's everything." That's all I could say. I didn't know how else to put into words what I thought about her. Lilly was everything.

"We have this connection. It's not romantic." Jeremiah sighed. "I can't explain it. She draws me in and makes me better," he said sincerely.

I understood. Lilly drew me in too, but it was more than romantic or sexual. She encouraged me to do what was right.

"Do you think it's a good idea for her to be in this big house all by herself? Especially after what happened to her parents and last night?"

"Obviously not. Which is why I'm going to stay here with her. Did your father know that you offered to have her stay with you?" Jeremiah asked.

I hesitated. I figured my father knew because Tucker had probably gone and run his mouth. I was surprised my father hadn't showed up on my doorstep.

"No."

"This isn't good. Any of it. She seems"—Jeremiah was thoughtful for a moment—"different. She won't back down. She'll die fighting for what she believes in."

"I know. That's why I wanted her staying with me. We need to keep her safe."

"At least we can agree on that," Jeremiah mumbled.

"She doesn't need any other distractions. Her safety is the

most important."

"You afraid she might take a liking to me?" Jeremiah propped himself against the wall.

He was goading me. Trying to get me to say what he'd obviously guessed at. That I wanted her.

"I have no idea what you're talking about," I grumbled, shoving my hands in my pockets. "I'm heading up to the attic to poke around." I stomped away, leaving Jeremiah laughing.

Maybe she would take a liking to Jeremiah. The situation would probably be better if she did. The way I felt about her was another scandal waiting to happen. At least I knew he'd keep her safe and be good to her. But I'd die a little every day watching them together. Just like I was dying a little bit now each time she showed him any affection.

I went into the attic hoping to find something. I wasn't sure what, a distraction from the thoughts of Jeremiah and Lilly?

I found a box of old photos, and although shuffling through them might have been pointless, they were a nice diversion from everything that had happened. Some of the photos had my father in them. He and Charles had been best friends growing up, so it wasn't out of the ordinary. It was comforting to see the pictures, to see a time when my father was so different. Earlier pictures of his teen years looked different. My father was visibly happier. He was smiling and his arm was wrapped around Charles. Later pictures were darker, though. Something had changed, and as I dug deeper into the photos, I found my father, more often than not, standing next to Charles with a scowl on his face, or off to the side, trying to hide himself from the picture. I guessed I was watching his downward spiral with each picture that I came across.

"What the hell?" I stopped at a photo of Iris holding a baby. The child was wrapped in blue, his face barely visible. The photo looked like it had been taken in my living room, and Iris sat in a chair that to this day, was placed right next to my fireplace. A man stood next to her, his arm wrapped around her shoulders. It was an intimate touch. He had pulled her closer to him, in a stance that clearly said he was claiming his property. My heart ached for Iris. Even though she smiled, it looked forced, and the grip of the fingers on her shoulder confirmed my suspicions. I looked more closely at the man who stood next to her, and I dropped the photo. I watched it drift to the ground as I felt disgust overtake me.

Chapter Twenty-seven: Lilly

1937

Just being close to Christopher sent me whirling with want and need that would have my fate sealed, just like my parents. I didn't want to be in this house by myself any more than he wanted me to be, but I couldn't be near him. I knew what would happen. Christopher seemed to have the same pull towards me that I had towards him. I'd seen his face when he walked in on me and Jeremiah. The relationship between Jeremiah and me wasn't romantic, though, and I wanted to scream that at Christopher and wrap my body around his. Have him rip the dress from my body, seam from seam, and make love to me like there were no barriers between us. To forget the pain of my parent's death, to say a solid *screw you* to society and their ideals that Christopher and I couldn't be.

After last night, and what had happened the other day at the ice cream parlor, I thought he knew that I wouldn't sit idly by while anyone threatened me. I knew that scared him and sometimes I wished I could just let the world hide behind a civility that didn't exist. I couldn't, though, and I wouldn't.

"Are you okay?" Jeremiah asked as he came up behind me while I breathed erratically and propped myself up against the wall. "I know all that's been going on is a lot to handle, but I won't let anything happen to you, you know that?"

I glanced up at Jeremiah. Did I know that? I barely knew him.

"I don't know you, or Christopher, or Virginia." I flung my

hands up in defeat. "But I want to believe you. God, do I." I shook my head. "I don't want anyone else to get hurt. This is my fight."

Jeremiah took my hand in his. "Hey." He brought his free hand to my face and tilted my chin. "This isn't your fight. You're here because your parents were murdered. It's more than that though. What you are fighting for is this for all of us."

I opened my mouth to say something when I heard Christopher clear his throat.

"I have something you might want to see." Christopher spoke directly to me, and Jeremiah released me and gave my hand a quick squeeze.

"What is it?" I asked curiously as I walked towards Christopher. There was a photograph in his hands.

"I'm not sure you're ready —?" Jeremiah scoffed and snatched the photo out of Christopher's hands. His demeanor changed, his body rigid.

"It was in a box in the attic," Christopher said as Jeremiah released the photo, sending it flitting to the ground like the petals of a flower.

"What is it?" I glanced between Jeremiah and Christopher. Jeremiah stormed off, running out of the house with a slam of the door.

I stared down the stairs, contemplating whether to run after him and console him, like he had done for me not too long before. As I started to move towards the stairs, Christopher pulled me back. Not just physically.

"Christopher," I whispered. His name fell from my lips like a promise I knew I couldn't keep.

"Don't go. Give him time."

I turned towards Christopher and our gaze connected. I studied him — deep into his face that was forbidden. His lips were pursed in a perfect little scowl. I assumed he was thinking that I was going to leave him and go after Jeremiah. As if he read my mind, Christopher pulled me into him, my chest resting against him. I stopped breathing and closed my eyes, willing this moment to never end. Because the moment held a promise. A promise that maybe, just maybe, what we felt could become something.

"Breathe, beautiful."

I let out a staggered breath and opened my eyes. Christopher stared down at me, his eyes conveying everything I'd been trying to avoid the days I had been here. The want, the need. Those feelings were there, fixed on me, on the person I hope he wanted. I wasn't another black woman who someone felt sorry for. There was no pity. In his eyes I saw respect. Desire. But most importantly, there was love. So much love. And suddenly I didn't care how wrong this was. In his arms, I knew I could find everything I had been missing.

"Can I kiss you?"

I smiled. He asked permission to kiss me? Such a gentleman. I wanted to say no, because I knew what would happen if anyone found out. I'd be shoved in prison, maybe worse. Same for Christopher. He was on the right side of the law, but the law still didn't favor my kind. My mind was trying to rationalize why this shouldn't happen, but my body called to him, spoke to him on a level that my mind couldn't push aside. I closed my eyes again and leaned forward, our lips brushing softly.

Christopher moaned against my mouth, and I opened it slightly, giving him access to all of me. As much as me as he could take. His tongue reached out, and swirling bliss hit me all the way to my core. I'd never been with a man before. Not fully anyway, but my body moved like it knew what it had to do. My hips instinctively rolled forward, feeling Christopher's arousal as it pressed against the fabric of my dress.

"Please. Make it all disappear." I pulled away and

whispered those words to him. A plea, a cry for help.

"Lilly, I'm not sure —" He held my arms and studied my face. It was as if he were looking for hesitation or any sign that I would regret this. But I didn't. I wouldn't. Christopher was everything I'd ever wanted. Everything I didn't know I wanted.

"I'm not sure what tomorrow is going to bring, Christopher, but I do know that you protected me last night. You held me close because you want this, too." I smiled. "Make love to me. Forget what everyone would say for a moment." I took his hand and placed it over my heart as I struggled to breathe. "Make me feel human. Make me feel wanted. Pretend my skin color doesn't matter. That what we feel for each other is more than skin deep." Tears fell down my cheeks.

Christopher brushed the tears away with one swift motion of his fingers. He placed his hands on the side of my cheeks and looked me in the eyes. God, he was beautiful. I knew it wasn't common to call a man beautiful, but Christopher, while he was strikingly handsome, was also more than that. It was his soul that had reached out to me from the first moment I saw him. His struggles were there, his hesitation with what was right, but inside, he was a man who wanted the world to change. A man who loved so fiercely, it threatened to kill us both. Now, here, with my lips inches from his, the consequences were nothing compared to a life of not knowing what this kind of love felt like. Everything my parents had fought for and lost — I understood it now. They had gained something far greater than many people ever experienced. They had gained their soul mate.

"Your skin color doesn't matter to me, Lilly. When I saw you that first day, I thought you were stunning. I wouldn't care if you were pink with polka dots."

I laughed in between the tears.

"Last night, I held you close because you're right and

beautiful, and what is going on is wrong. All of it is wrong. I don't give a crap what anyone says about us, because this is real. It is more than skin deep." And with those words, he lifted me into his arms and held me close to his chest. I rested my head against him as he carried me into the bedroom then shut the door. Gently, he placed me on the bed and stood over me. I looked at him, and any hesitation that I had was now a distant memory. It was us now. Just us. No others.

He slowly removed his shirt, and I couldn't take my eyes off him. His muscles, his body, the perfection that was Christopher Weatherby. I moved my hands to my dress buttons, and he shook his head.

"Let me." He motioned for me to stand. His hands were quick, as they released each button on my dress. I let the garment fall to the ground, leaving me exposed in nothing but my bra and underwear.

"You're the most gorgeous woman I've ever laid eyes on, Lilly Porter," he said with a smile. Walking behind me, he kissed my neck and whispered words that made me weak at the knees. Promises that he'd never leave. Promises that what we shared, even though we just met, was real, so real.

I removed my bra and it fell to the ground, joining my dress. Christopher went back in front of me and bent over slightly, taking my nipple in his mouth. Nibbles, bites, tugs — the sensations made pools of moisture form between my legs. I let out soft moans with each touch of his fingers, with each brush of his mouth against my overheated skin.

"Do you like that, Lilly?" he asked through a mouthful of my nipple.

"Yes," I said only somewhat coherently.

He slid further down my body and removed my panties in one quick motion. He laid me on the bed, and I took in a breath. This was it. I was going to give myself completely to the man who had stolen my heart in just a short period of time. I was never more sure about anything in my entire life. I smiled as he unzipped his pants, but he stopped, his face turning more serious.

"Are you nervous?" He held his pants together.

I wanted nothing more than for him to let his pants fall so I could see all of him. "I trust you."

With that, Christopher took his delectable lips that had kissed every inch of my body and pressed them down on mine.

"I'll be gentle. I promise." He undid his pants, and they fell to the floor to join the tangled mess of the rest of our clothes. He was rock hard, and from the moisture that gathered at the tip of him, I knew he was as excited as I was. Placing his arms on either side of me, Christopher straddled me with his legs. "It'll hurt, only for minute." His words brushed against my ear.

I didn't say anything. There was nothing to say. I wasn't a fragile doll who needed to be handled with care. I wanted Christopher, and trickles of my desire slid down my legs, making my body ready for him too.

"Make love to me," I pleaded as Christopher's heavy, staggered breath brushed against my ear. "Please." I wanted his resolve.

With one gentle motion, Christopher was inside me. I felt a sting, and I held back the groan that lingered on the tip of my tongue. It hurt only for a second, but each thrust, each roll of hips, was better than the last.

"Are you okay?" Christopher asked breathlessly as I moaned and moved underneath him.

I wasn't moving out of pain but into feelings of pleasure I had never imagined. I smiled wide as I wrapped my legs around him, pushing my hips forward to meet Christopher's thrusts. I wanted him as deep as possible. I didn't want anything held back. I grasped his arms as our bodies slid against each other Every single nerve ending in my body was feeling the intensity. His breathing, his kisses, even his soft moans made me want to lose control.

I was catapulting out of control, spinning into an abyss that could only be described as heaven. Christopher took the pad of his thumb and rubbed it against a part of me that sent me whirling.

"Oh, God." My head rolled back as my body tightened and convulsed around him. My vision became blurry, and my body limp as my muscles let loose their tension. But Lord, was I flying high. With another thrust, Christopher spewed profanities as he collapsed on top of me, brushing kisses across my face.

When we were finally able to compose ourselves, we lay next to each other, staring at the ceiling and reveling in the moment. Christopher reached over and took my hand in his. And that was the way we stayed until I drifted off into a peaceful sleep. No worries, no fears, just us, finally giving into our feelings.

"What the hell? You slept with her?"

I gasped and pulled the blanket over me. Jeremiah stood in the doorway. Christopher jumped up, all of his manhood on display.

"Jeremiah, calm down." Christopher put up his hands.

Jeremiah stormed in and threw Christopher's clothes at him.

"How could you?" Jeremiah yelled.

"Enough!" I sat up. "I'm not yours, Jeremiah. He didn't make me. I wanted it. I wanted it more than you'll ever know." I looked at Christopher, and he smiled at me.

"You are mine, Lilly. You're all I have left. I have to protect you," Jeremiah said as he fell to the ground, covering his face with his hands.

"What do you mean all you have left?" I stood, draping the sheet around me, covering my nakedness.

"You're my sister. I won't let anything happen to you."

I let out a small gasp. A brother. *I have a brother?* How was that possible? Jeremiah looked at me, the sadness gone and replaced with almost one of acceptance on his face. Christopher moved towards me and held out the photograph from earlier that I hadn't gotten a chance to see. I focused on an image of my mother holding an infant boy in her arms Flipping it over, I read —

My precious one. Jeremiah and his father

The man next to her wasn't my father, though. It was Christopher's, his arm draped around her possessively. I couldn't get enough air. My chest heaved as I struggled to get air into my lungs.

"Oh, my God." I managed to breathe out. Everything turned hazy. I saw Jeremiah and Christopher's mouths moving but heard nothing. All I remembered was Jeremiah and Christopher rushing towards me as I fell to the floor and everything went black.

CHAPTER TWENTY-EIGHT: CHARLES

1912

Looking at myself in the mirror, there was no pride or excitement. I was twenty-three now, half a year away from having my college degree and being a lawyer. All my other friends were out celebrating their college break, getting married, and starting to settle down. I was trying to figure out how I was going to be able to marry the woman I loved.

I hadn't seen Iris yet. I'd been home only a few hours and strategically trying to avoid her. It was difficult because I was drawn to her, like a bee to honey. She was a part of me, an extension of myself. When I saw her, I wanted to tell her I had answers. That she and I could be together. In order to do that, I had to talk with my father. I straightened out my tie and headed to his office where I knew he'd be.

I knocked at the door, my palms sweaty and my heart beating erratically in my chest.

"Come in."

As I opened the door, it was heavy against my hands, grounding me, and I held it tight. I was scared.

My father glanced up from his paperwork and gave me a curt smile.

"Welcome back, Son." He motioned for me to sit across from him.

I sat and ran my fingers through my hair.

"You all right? You look a little pale." He put his pen down.

My father barely paid any attention to me. Except for when

it benefited him. I was one of the top students in my college class, which reflected nicely on my father. Hence, the reason why I was probably getting the time of day right now.

"I need to talk to you."

He frowned and stood, walking towards the window.

"I um . . ." My words wouldn't come out.

Jesus, just tell him!

"Oh, get on with it, Charles!" He threw up his arms in frustration.

I took a deep breath.

"I fell in love." I took another breath. "I mean, I don't want to. I am. I've fallen in love." I waited for my father to say something.

He smiled and came towards me, smacking me on my back. "That's great, son." He laughed.

I furrowed my brow. "What's so funny?" I sat up straighter.

"Fredrick. He came here a few months ago ranting and raving about you and Iris. I knew he was going crazy. Spending too much time with those white supremacists. "

"Father . . ."

He stopped talking and looked at me, the relief in his eyes slowly washing away. "It is her, isn't it?" His voice was low and calm.

I was relieved about that. My father was never the most approachable man, but I didn't want to slither away. I didn't want to run. Iris was not a woman to be hidden. I loved her with a fierceness that burned stronger every day. I wasn't going to be a coward and run without telling my father how I felt. Owning up to my love of a woman who deserved everything in the world, not the life that she was born into.

"Ah, Charles." My father slammed his fists onto the desk. I never heard my father swear or lose control. "You can't be with her. You can't."

Now was my chance. My chance to do what was right. I

stood.

"I will. And I can." My voice was shaky, but the words, they were the truth. "After I finish this last semester, we're moving to Philadelphia. I'm going to start my own practice out there."

He slumped in his chair.

"I respect you, father. I didn't want to just run away without telling you."

The silence was deafening. He stared at me.

"I know this isn't what you want for me."

He held up his hand. "Enough, son." He sighed. "You're right. This isn't what I want for you. I wanted you to marry a nice woman and take over the family firm. I wanted you to give me grandchildren with your mother's blonde hair and blue eyes."

I stiffened at the mention of my mother. We never talked about her, ever.

"I—"

"Let me finish," he said interrupting me once again. "You have always followed what I wanted. Especially since your mother died. She would be proud of you."

A single tear escaped my eye. This wasn't how I was expecting this to go. I was expecting to be cast out and told to never come back.

"I'm proud of you."

I choked. He was proud of me? He wasn't going to throw me out?

"I can't support you openly. It'll kill my creditability around here. But I won't stop you." He stood then put his hand on my shoulder. "I'm happy you found love, son. I'll finish paying for your college and give you your inheritance."

I didn't want his money.

"Let me do that for you. Let me help you get your life set up. It's the least I can do when I can't be as brave as you."

All I could do was nod. I didn't know what to say. How to form into words how grateful I was for my father's support. I'd grown up afraid of him and his terse and unapproachable nature. He was only human, though. Just like Iris and me.

"I'm so proud of you, son." He hugged me. One of the only hugs I remember getting from my father.

I left his office more hopeful than I'd ever been. I ran through the house looking for Iris. I smiled, realizing she was probably down by the lake, soaking up the few minutes of free time she had. I couldn't wait to tell her, that nothing could stand in our way. Not anymore. Soon, we would be free.

Chapter Twenty-nine: Christopher

1937

I held Lilly in my arms while Jeremiah paced back and forth. Her breaths were short and steady, and there was a little scowl that furrowed her brow. I couldn't help but smile.

"I shouldn't have told her like that." Jeremiah punched the wall. "I'm an idiot."

"It's okay. You were in shock over the news, too. She had to find out somehow." I brushed some hair that had fallen into her face so I could fully see her.

"I've got a sister." Jeremiah smiled and stopped to take a glimpse of Lilly.

"And a brother. Two of them." I looked up at him.

He nodded, the hardness in his face disappearing for a minute. We had grown up together, Jeremiah and I. We always had a close relationship, and now I knew why. We were brothers.

"What?" Tucker stood in the doorway his teeth clenched together as he gazed at Lilly in my arms. "What the hell is going on here?"

I brought Lilly closer to my chest, and she let out a small moan.

"Tucker, calm down." Jeremiah moved towards him and put his hand on Tucker's chest.

"Why is she wrapped in that sheet? Did you touch her, Christopher?"

I didn't say anything, I sat there. He barreled towards me

and tried to rip her out of my arms.

"You touch her, and I'll kill you." These words had been what I'd wanted to say last night. To tell all those assholes that had come here fishing for trouble. I was scared then. But not anymore. I'd had a taste of Lilly, and I never wanted anything else. "What the hell are you doing here anyways?"

"I came once I heard what happened last night. Sucks about those graves." He smiled, and I wanted nothing more than to punch him in the face.

"It is. They laid their hands on her. You laid your hands on her. Don't do it again. I meant what I said. I will kill you or anyone else who tries to hurt her."

"You'd choose that girl over me? Your brother?" Tucker scoffed.

"I'd choose Lilly and our brother, Jeremiah, over you any day." I placed Lilly on the bed and then handed Tucker the picture.

All went silent in the room as he looked at it. I knew he wouldn't be accepting of it, so I was still standing protectively over Lilly. He flipped the photo over and read what Lilly had, not that long prior. He crumbled the photo in his hands and threw it across the room.

"Our father slept with Iris," Jeremiah said.

"He did something with Iris. It wasn't consensual." Virginia stood in the hallway.

I forgot she was still here from last night. I was glad she'd missed what just happened.

"What do you mean?" Jeremiah asked.

"Iris was my daughter. She was raised by my sister and put back in my care when she was old enough to serve."

I let a tiny smile spread across my face and glanced back at Lilly. She wasn't alone. She had a brother and a grandmother, all who no doubt loved her and would care for her. And she had me. She'd always have me.

"So?" Tucker shrugged.

"Your father raped her when he found out Charles and Iris were in love and wanted to leave."

Jeremiah fell into the chair, and my entire body went rigid. "My father raped a woman?

"My father hates blacks. He wouldn't touch them," Tucker argued.

"He loved Iris, honey," Virginia said to Tucker through her tears. "He didn't know how to handle those emotions because . . . think of all those years ago and how things were."

Tucker stared blankly at her.

"Iris loved Charles, though, and Charles wasn't afraid of anything. All he needed was her."

"My father raped my mother?" Jeremiah had tears streaming down his face. I squeezed his shoulder. A small token of comfort for what he had just found out. I wanted the hate, the knowledge of what my father did to Iris to stay with me. Because I was going to have a talk with my father, and he was going to answer for what he had done.

"I don't believe any of this shit. You're a liar. Trying to slander my family's name." Tucker stormed towards Virginia, and Jeremiah and I both sprung up, protectively standing around her.

"Don't do it, brother," Jeremiah said.

"I am not your brother. You half-breed." Tucker rubbed his face hard and shook his head. "It's unnatural!" He ran down the stairs then slammed the door, leaving me in a state of shock.

Lilly rustled, released some small moans, and after some stretching, she opened her eyes. She sat up slowly, looking at Virginia, Jeremiah, and me.

"What did I miss?" she asked.

We all laughed painfully.

I sat next to her and gently pressed my lips to hers. I didn't care anymore. Forbidden or not, I wouldn't hide my feelings any longer. I'd be like Charles and accept what was being offered. We all had a right to choose and I chose acceptance and love. I chose Lilly.

Jeremiah coughed, and I gave him a smile.

"That's my sister," he said somewhat playfully. I knew he meant it, though. Despite just finding out who Lilly truly was to him, Jeremiah would protect her above all else. Even from me.

"A brother," Lilly whispered.

"You not only have a brother, but a grandmother as well."

Lilly's wiped her teared filled eyes before jumping up and running towards Virginia and Jeremiah. I watched them hug, laugh and cry. With all the awful things that had happened to her parents, the tragedy brought about a family that Lilly didn't even know she had. A family that had been with me all along. There was no doubt in my mind that Lilly and I were made to be together. I hoped we would be able to live out our life in peace and not meet the same fate as her parents.

CHAPTER THIRTY: IRIS

1912

I sat by the lake as I often did when I had a minute to myself. Things had been hard these past months waiting for Charles to come back from college. I tried to hold on to the memories, to the promise of a long happy life filled with laughter, happiness, and children. He'd be home soon for a break, and I couldn't wait to see him, to touch him, to feel him against me. There was something about holding the one you loved. It made everything else melt away. I was reading a letter he had sent home. It had been addressed to my mother, but she gave it to me. She protected our love. She hid it from everyone.

The letter was the only thing I had of Charles, the words he had written only for me. The happiness and longing he had poured onto the pages. I held Charles in my hands.

"Iris?" I glanced up from under the tree, and there was Fredrick, his hands shoved awkwardly in his pockets. He never came around anymore. He had become infatuated with becoming the mayor of Kittrell and was learning the ropes. After our kiss, things had been off anyways.

"Hi, Fredrick." I gave him a friendly smile and shoved the letter in my shirt before he could notice. Fredrick was Charles' best friend, but neither of us knew where his mind was. We had heard he was running with the wrong crowd. That he was supporting their mission full force. I didn't want to risk anything, so I kept my letter and my love for Charles hidden.

"You okay?" Fredrick said as he kicked rocks, making his

way over to me then sat down. This seemed normal. Like how things used to be, where we would all sit and talk about our hopes and dreams and a life away from Kittrell.

"Just thinking," I murmured.

Fredrick stared out at the water. It was all so peaceful. Too peaceful. What did he want? Maybe I was being paranoid.

"About Charles?"

My breath hitched in my throat as I thought of what to say.

"It's okay. It's been written all over your face since you two met." He laughed. "And when you smacked me for kissing you."

I tugged on my dress. I was beginning to become unsettled. Fredrick's demeanor was quickly changing.

"It's always been him, hasn't it?" His eyes bore into mine.

Gone was the serene lake and my thoughts of Charles. I was scared.

"It isn't that simple," I spoke up, my voice shaky.

He smiled at my discomfort and lunged forward, pinning me back against the tree. Fredrick shoved his hand in my shirt, pulling out the letter.

What could I do? I could try to get it back. Pointless. Fredrick outweighed me by probably 100 pounds. I had no options. None.

Fredrick read the letter, sweat beading on his forehead. Our entire life was planned out in that letter. Our secrets, our hopes, and our dreams.

"Funny how he thinks he can take his black girlfriend and just run away." Fredrick crumpled up the letter and tossed it into the lake.

Tears silently fell down my cheeks.

He pulled me up off the ground and crashed his lips down on mine. It was different than when he'd tried to kiss me before. The passion was gone. The feeling behind the kiss was laced with hate.

When he finally stopped kissing me, I tasted copper in my mouth. And the rest, I'd rather forget. But no matter how much I closed my eyes and tried to silence the sounds. He'd taken something from me — something I'd never get back.

"Iris?"

I don't know how long I'd been lying there. Was I dreaming? Did I hear Charles' voice?

"Iris?"

I opened my eyes. It was him.

"Charles!" I cried out. The trees rustled as I tried to sit up. I managed to prop myself against the tree.

Then I saw him. The man I loved. He looked at me with such sadness, such rage that I had to close my eyes again. I didn't want him to see me like this. Vulnerable, broken, abused. I was strong. Always.

Charles' hands were on my face and he held me close, whispering soothing words to me as he rocked me to and fro. He didn't ask what had happened. He didn't have to. He knew.

"It's going to be okay, Iris. I'll kill him. I'll kill him for what he did to you."

"No!" I said calmly. "Violence isn't going to solve this. It's never the answer."

Charles stood and glared down at me. "How can you say that, Iris? He violated you. He hurt you."

I smiled knowingly at him. "Fredrick may have hurt me Charles. He may have taken something from me. But you know what?" I paused and reached my hand out to him. He placed his hand in mine and squeezed. "He will never have my heart or my love. No matter what. My heart and love are yours. Only yours."

Charles cried. I was angry for what Fredrick had taken from me, but more so, I was sad that he felt he had to. He could have let me go, but his pride, the lessons he learned from his own father made him see me, someone who was once his friend, as something to be possessed.

"I'm going to walk back to the house now. I'm sure there are things for me to do." I kissed Charles' cheek.

As I made my way towards the house, Fredrick stood in the doorway, his arms crossed.

I fought back bile as he gripped my arm, bringing his mouth close to my ear.

I remembered what it all felt like. How I begged and pleaded for him to stop. But he didn't. I didn't fight. I could have, but where would that have gotten me? Further from Charles, from the man I loved.

"I'll always be a part of you now, Iris. Nine months from now, that baby that you have . . . That bastard will be mine." He smiled at me. "You will not speak of this to anyone. I will raise the kid, but every day I will make their life a living hell and there is nothing you can do about it."

I whimpered.

"Because, if you say anything, I'll kill Charles. I'll kill your mother. But I'll leave you alive so you can experience the pain every day. Like I have to." He spat on my dress. "I could have been a good man to you. You would have served me well. But you messed that up and had to fall in love with my best friend. It could have been me. It should have been me!" he yelled.

He stormed off, leaving me with the reminder of what happened and his promise. Maybe I wouldn't get pregnant. Maybe I wouldn't have to hand over my child to this monster. Maybe the dreams in the letter that Charles wrote to me would come true.

I closed my eyes and walked into the house, to my responsibilities, hoping that things would turn out okay.

Nine months later, I handed over my son to my mother.

"Please, Fredrick, don't make me leave him."

Fredrick looked sad. Deep down I saw the sadness as I held onto my son for dear life. There was that little boy under the façade, the one who had sat by the lake with Charles and me all those years ago. He wanted to be that boy. I saw it in his eyes when I handed my son over to my mother. He glanced down at him and a flicker of pride danced across his face.

It was quickly replaced with hate as he stood in the doorway to his house. Charles and I stood hand and hand.

"I loved you Iris, and you disregarded me." He laughed. "All my friends are right. You are all horrible, useless human beings." Fredrick turned to Charles. "And you, you're worse than all of them. A damn sympathizer."

"Let us take the boy. You don't even want him," Charles said, holding my hand tightly.

"No!" Fredrick yelled. "I don't want him. You're right." Then, he smiled, and it chilled me. "I wanted her." He pointed to me. "And now, every day, she will remember what she had to give up." He ripped Jeremiah from my mother's arms and held him close. "Leave before I tell everyone. You'll both be dead."

I sobbed as Charles dragged me away.

As I stole glances of my son, Fredrick watched me, the cunning smile never leaving his face as he held our son in his arms. At least my son was alive. Because I knew Fredrick would hold true to his promise. He'd kill everyone I loved just to prove a point. And if anyone found out about Charles and me, we'd be punished to the full extent of the law.

I realized something the night I handed over my son. I had told Charles that Fredrick would never have my heart or my love, because it was all for him. That was true, I'd never love another man like I loved Charles. But leaving my son with Fredrick, I left a part of my heart and my love with my son,

Jeremiah, and I knew I'd never get it back.

CHAPTER THIRTY-ONE: LILLY

1937

Who knew that with such sadness I could find such hope? As I sat and talked with my grandmother and brother, it took away some of the pain. I knew it'd be short lived, but I relished the time I had with them now. Because something this good wasn't meant to last—a storm was coming Was that why my parents were killed so young? Because they had a good thing?

I glanced over at Christopher as he watched me closely. We had a good thing. I clenched my thighs together, the pleasurable soreness of how great of a thing we had radiating over my body. I didn't want it to end. Ever. I couldn't imagine how all of this was impacting him. He'd learned about what his father did, not only the rape, but making my mother give up her son.

"Your mom loved you, Jeremiah. She didn't want to leave, but Fredrick made her leave you with me and him or he'd . . ." Virginia stopped as Jeremiah jumped up.

"I can't hear anymore. I can't hear about what an awful man my father is. I'd rather have not known he was my father than have to live with what he did to my mother, what he did to you." He shook his head. Jeremiah's reaction was normal anger and sadness.

But Christopher showed no emotion. We all looked at him as he sat oddly still and quiet in the corner. He didn't move, and he hadn't spoken a word throughout the entire conversation.

"What?" Christopher asked as we all stared at him.

"You don't have anything to say about any of it?" I was the first to speak to him.

"What is there to say? I lived my whole life letting my father treat Jeremiah like trash. My own fucking brother!" Christopher stood and paced the floor. "God, I was an idiot. I thought that he kept Jeremiah around because of Virginia or something. But he always hated Jeremiah more than anyone else."

Jeremiah hung his head and averted all eye contact, clearly upset at Christopher's words.

"He beat him, for no reason sometimes. And now I know why. Because Jeremiah was a constant reminder of what he had done. The rape of an innocent woman all because she loved someone else. Because he couldn't handle loving a black woman."

"Son . . ." Virginia went towards Christopher, but he held up his hand, backing away.

"I need to be by myself right now." He walked out of room, leaving the rest of us to process the information alone.

We all sat in silence for a few minutes.

"Tell me about her."

I looked over at Jeremiah.

"Tell me about our mother."

This I knew. I knew our mother, and I knew her well. "She was outspoken and passionate about everything she did." I smiled, remembering her wanting only the best education for me. Arguing with the school board about why I should go to one school over the other. "And she knew how to love. She taught me how to be strong, how to work hard, and how to love everyone. Even when those people were spouting hate and ignorance."

"She sounds like a strong woman."

I moved closer to Jeremiah. "She was strong. She'd be proud of you." I placed my hand on his knee.

"Did she ever talk about me?"

The question stirred something in me. I briefly recalled a day that I was a little girl, and I found my mother crying when I came home from school.

"She didn't."

Jeremiah's face fell.

"She thought about you a lot, though. Now that I know more about her past, what she went through, it all makes sense. Iris was a wonderful mother, but she suffered every day that you weren't with her. I see that now."

"Momma! Where are you?" I padded through the house calling my mother's name. She was always here when I got home from school, standing at the kitchen counter making me a snack or waiting on the porch looking happy to see me. Not today. When I opened the door to my house the air felt different. Stuffy, full of regret and loneliness. I placed my bag on the counter and searched for my mother.

I ran up the stairs, my feet hitting the wooden floor hard. I saw the crack of my mother's bedroom door, her body hunched over on the bed, my father held her as he often did, rubbing her back. This seemed different, though. He whispered soothing words and brushed back her hair as he rocked her in his arms.

"It's okay, Iris."

"He'd be 11 today, Charles." She glanced up at my father, tears streaming down her face "He's turning into a man and doesn't even know I exist."

My dad kissed her forehead and didn't say anything. Who was she talking about? I moved closer to the door so I could hear more of their conversation. The floorboards creaked and my parents turned and faced me.

"Lilly." My mom brushed away her tears, masking the pain with the smile that she greeted me with every day. "Let's go down to the

kitchen and I'll fix you a snack."

My mother took my hand in hers and hummed. Every day she hummed, she soothed my worries and she encouraged me. But now I knew my mother kept something close to her. A past and secrets that I didn't know. As I glanced back at father, who still sat on the bed, he cupped his face in his hands. The strongest man I'd even known wept into his hands. I squeezed my mother's hand tighter that day, wishing that I could take all their pain away.

"I thought she forgot about me," Jeremiah said as he wiped away the tears that had fallen while I told him about my memory.

"Never. I didn't know then what had them both so sad. They were wonderful parents, but what happened here in Kittrell changed them, Jeremiah." I reached out and patted his hand. "She left a piece of herself here that night she left you."

"She came here, you know. Before they died."

I wasn't shocked by Jeremiah's confession. My mother loved him. A son she never knew. It made sense that she'd try to see him, no matter how dangerous it was.

"Really? Did you say anything to her?"

Jeremiah shook his head. "No, But I remembered her face, from when I was little. I saw a picture once, on Fredrick's desk." He let out a small laugh. "Guess I know why he kept that picture of her. Then that day that she and Charles were taken, I saw her. She stood staring at Christopher's house for what seemed liked forever. Charles came behind her and wrapped his arms around her, and she fell to the ground crying." Jeremiah stood up. "Now I know why."

Secrets were being revealed, and the life my parents had led before having me was coming to light. Yet, I still felt unsettled, like something was missing.

"It's going to be okay, right, Jeremiah?" I don't know why I suddenly had such doubt and fear in how this all would end, but knowing now that my mother was raped, that Mayor

Weatherby was to blame for that, I had little hope that we'd all walk away unscathed.

"I don't know, Lilly." He sighed. "I wish I could offer you comfort, but Christopher won't be able to let this go. I can't let this go. Any of it. Someone is going to have to pay."

I didn't know what to do. I wanted someone to pay too. But at what cost? Who had to die for justice to be served? From what had happened since I'd arrived, I knew violence was the way here. In just a few days, I had gained so much. Now I was afraid to lose it.

"I can't lose you or Virginia."

"Or Christopher," Jeremiah added with a smile. Before I could respond, pounding at the front door ended our conversation.

"Will someone get the door for me please?" Virginia yelled from downstairs.

"Who could that be?"

Jeremiah and I headed to the door. I was apprehensive about what I was going to find on the other side, and Jeremiah gave me a reassuring nod.

My brother.

That was our connection from the beginning. I wasn't alone the night I buried my parents—my brother and grandmother had stood beside me. The realization brought me a sense of comfort in the aftermath of my grief. I wasn't alone after all.

I peered through the peep hole to be safe. "Scarlett?" I opened the door and motioned her inside. "What are you doing here?"

"Oh, honey." She pulled me in for a hug.

Jeremiah walked away, knowing now that no one was here to pick a fight.

"I came as soon as I heard what happened. Was anyone hurt?"

I stood and stared at Scarlett. She came because she was

worried?

"Where's the Sheriff? I heard he was here." She glanced around.

"He's here. Somewhere," I mumbled. "Please come in. Do you want some sweet tea or something?" I led the way to the sitting room.

"That'd be great." Her high heels clacked against the hardwood floors. She wore another flashy dress, this one a bright blue, and she had on matching nail polish. Her heels where much higher than I'd ever dream to wear, and their bright white flashed in dramatic comparison to her dress.

"I wanted you to know that I am here for you." Scarlett sat on the couch, and I sat on the oversized chair across from her.

"I know people here haven't been the nicest but that isn't me." She sat straighter. "My parents raised me right."

"I appreciate that. It's nice to know I have someone here."

"You've got me," Jeremiah said as he walked in with some drinks. He set them down on the table as Scarlett looked between us, confused.

"Are you two a thing?" Scarlett asked. "Geez, I've been trying to snag me a Weatherby for years, and you come in and get a man in only a few days." She laughed.

When she'd mentioned the first day how the Weatherby men were attractive, I hadn't noticed the glint in her eye. But today, it was there. She was serious. She wanted a Weatherby, and that included Christopher. I brushed my fingers against my lips remembering the kisses we'd shared, the way his teeth grazed my nipples.

"No!"

Jeremiah's voice took me out of my daydream. He made a face and went back into the kitchen. I thought about whether I should tell Scarlett about Jeremiah being my brother. I glanced over at her as she sipped her sweet tea and smiled at me. I needed a friend. Someone besides Christopher who'd left without a word.

"Jeremiah's my brother."

Scarlett set her glass down gently and looked up at me. "How is that possible? Your mother and father had Jeremiah and left him here?" She tilted her head to the side.

"No. Someone else is his father. My mother was raped."

Scarlett leaned forward and put her hand on my leg. "I'm sorry, sweetie. Do you know who it is? Who raped your mother?"

Her simple gesture of kindness made my eyes well up with tears. I knew who had raped my mother. I knew where he lived and what he stood for. The hate and lies. I nodded.

"It's okay to cry. That's an awful thing to find out in light of everything else that has happened." Her words were sincere and fueled me to continue talking.

"I have to be strong. To stand on my own two feet and push back my own problems and emotions to figure this all out. So, my parents get justice."

Scarlett looked at me thoughtfully. "Emotions can help guide you to where you need to go. They can be good. If you allow them to be."

I let my tears fall.

"Thanks, Scarlett. Your words mean a lot to me."

She smiled and got up, moving towards the door. "I must head out, but I just wanted to check on you. I know we don't know each other well, but I'm here if you need me." She brought me in for a hug. I softened against her and for the first time since last night, I felt better. Maybe all that I needed was in front of me, my family, a new friend. They'd all be there to help me through this and make sure I came out okay.

Chapter Thirty-two: Iris

1937

"I've got to do this, Charles. I need to see my son."

Charles kissed my forehead as he took my hand in his. Charles wasn't any regular man. He was understanding and kind. He was, without a doubt, the love of my life.

"I can't promise you if Fredrick is there, I won't punch him in the face." He smiled coyly. "I should have done that decades ago, when he raped you and took Jeremiah away from us."

The guilt on his face tore me into pieces. Charles would have taken the sun from the sky if I asked. But I didn't believe in violence, even though it would have given me immense satisfaction to see harm come to Fredrick over what he did to me. I knew violence wasn't the way. It was never the way.

"We both could have done a lot differently back then. Times were worse then, Charles. Change is coming ... slowly, but it's coming." He nodded.

"Let's go see your son."

When we pulled up to Fredrick's house, nothing much had changed. All the memories came flooding back, like a bad dream that had been on repeat my entire life. I slowly got out of the car, asking Charles to stay behind, so I could see and talk to Jeremiah myself.

As I moved closer to the door, the curtain at the window from upstairs shifted. Then I saw him, my boy. He wasn't a boy anymore. His was tall, handsome, and looked so much like me. I had missed him. I should have saved him, fought harder to keep him with me. What kind of mother left her own son in the hands of a man who was capable of such evil? I collapsed to the ground with my grief and guilt.

"I've got you, Iris. It's going to be okay." Charles and I sat on the ground, my back against him as he let me cry for my son and a childhood I suspected wasn't kind to him. I had failed him as a mother. I couldn't protect him from the hate that festered in his father. That was why I'd wanted to protect Lilly so fiercely. If I could protect her from it, maybe I'd be able to find peace in that. But I hadn't. The guilt still crept in, every chance it could.

"Don't fucking move."

Charles went rigid against my back. This was it. The hate had found us. I glanced back up at the window, Jeremiah was gone. I said a silent prayer that he didn't have to bear witness to what was going to happen.

I stood. My hand intertwined with Charles'. I placed a kiss to his lips — the last touch of his lips I'd ever know.

"I love you, Charles." With a gun positioned to the back of our heads, we went to meet our fates. The fate that we had run from our entire lives.

Chapter Thirty-three: Christopher

1937

"Lilly?"

I'd been down by the lake all day and most of the night. I ruminated on every word of our conversation. I couldn't face anyone. Not even myself. I knew my father was an asshole racist but hearing that he had raped Lilly's mother stirred something inside me that I hadn't even known was there. Hate. A hate so deep that it threatened to strangle me, and anyone in my way.

Now it coursed through me like a sickness, and I didn't know how to stop it. Violence. That was the only thing that kept popping into my head. I wanted to barrel through my father's front door, drag him out, and tie him to the same tree that Iris had been tied to. I wanted him to feel what it was like to be afraid. The violence that swirled around my mind wasn't me, so I went for a drive, a long drive to clear my head. As the miles passed by, the scenery flashed past. The silhouette of Lilly's body in the bed, long and sleek, invaded my thoughts. All the emotions from earlier came surfacing back and I was overcome with the need to be next to her. I wanted her body against mine. I imagined her smiling face, the gentle caress on my cheek from the kiss she stole. She was my savior.

I took off my shirt and pants, tossing them on the floor with Lilly's clothes. I crept into bed, and gently moved back the covers. She moaned, a glorious sound that went straight through me.

I let my hands graze over her stomach, the soft malleable flesh igniting my body. She moaned again and arched her back, pressing her ass against my erection. Even in sleep her body responded to my touch.

"Christopher?" Her voice was low, a need filled whisper as I pressed myself against her.

"Stay just like this."

She complied, letting her head roll back and rest against the pillow. I moved my hand down further and stopped right at the beginning of her center. I played there for a few minutes, tracing and touching her. Her eyes were still closed, but she rolled her hips against my hand.

I couldn't take it anymore. I needed to be inside her. I needed to get lost in the moment and bury all the thoughts I had. I lifted the fabric of her nightgown and pressed my myself against her backside. Lilly turned to face me, a look of concern in her eyes. I didn't need that now. I didn't need her sympathy.

"We need to talk," she said. I took her chin in my hands and pressed my lips against hers.

"I know. We will, but please, not yet. I need this."

Her look turned thoughtful. There it was, the permission I needed to take what I wanted.

I rolled on top of her and with one quick motion I removed her nightgown. In the darkness, it was difficult to see all of her. The outline of her breasts was visible, and I bit down on one of her nipples. She screeched, and it made me even harder. I took two fingers and gently slid them inside her. She was already wet for me. I moved my fingers in and out with ease as I continued to play with her breasts with my teeth and tongue. She writhed underneath me, flailing as I pleased her with my fingers. I liked being in control, watching her lose herself to my touch.

"Stop," Lilly said breathlessly.

I released my fingers, and her juices dripped down my hand. I loved the way her body responded to me. After only one time together, she knew me, wanted me, like I wanted her.

"Are you okay?" I asked.

She sat up and pushed me back on the bed.

"What?" My gaze found hers as she straddled me. I saw her perfectly now, the reflection from the light of the moon dancing on her beautiful skin. Her hair hung loose around her shoulders, the sleep gone from her face.

"I'm going to make you forget," she whispered against my lips before flicking her tongue into my mouth. She kissed me, fisting me, she gripped harder each time she swirled her tongue in my mouth. My excitement gathered at the tip of my penis, and she used it as lubrication to continue stroking me with her hand. Her touch was like magic, each pump of her fist sent me further and further gone. She had me, mind and body. All there was, was Lilly and me.

She let go of me and released her lips from mine. My lips throbbed with pleasure, the blood pooling there from the passionate kissing we had shared. With her legs braced on either side of me she lowered herself—the most wonderful slick sound filling the room. I moaned, digging my fingers into her hips. Her soft flesh molded to my hands and I held her, guiding her thrusts, the motion of her hips as she rode me.

I grabbed her tightly pulling her closer to me and thrust myself deeper into her. I'd be more than just her first, I'd be her only.

"Is that okay?" Lilly moaned as I plunged into her.

I hissed. It was more than okay; it was heaven. "It's amazing. Keep going." I gripped her hips harder, and she sucked in a sharp breath as she positioned herself up on her feet, squatting on top of me. And then she did it. The wonderful brazen woman that Lilly was crashed herself down on me over and over again. That was all I needed, watching her breasts bounce up and down. I came, hard and fast as she rode me slowly.

She rolled off me, breathing heavily.

I turned towards her and sprinkled kissed on her face. I didn't want this moment to end. Thoughts of Lilly and me to-gether, happy and away from this mess came into my mind. We could move anywhere. Go someplace where we could be together without fear.

"We still need to talk," she whispered against my mouth.

I laughed. "About last night?" I questioned bringing her into my arms.

"Yes. You left. I didn't know where you went. After what happened between us, I thought maybe you . . ."

"Never." I looked down at her. "Never would I regret a moment with you Lilly." She breathed out.

"What are we going to do?" Lilly asked into my chest.

"We're going to make my father pay for what he did. I think he knows who murdered your parents."

Lilly sat up. "But he's your father."

The sheet fell from around her exposing her breasts. I kneaded one of them.

"Stop distracting me!" She swatted my hand away.

"It calms me." I groaned and dropped my hand to my side. I pulled her back on my chest and smoothed her hair. "He is my father, Lilly. Nothing will ever change that. But what he did was wrong, and I know now that he was likely behind what happened to your parents. I'm going to make him pay . . . Justice is best served swift and with unwavering judgement. If he was anyone else, I would have hauled him in already. Tomorrow morning, I'm going to him and we'll find out once and for all what happened."

Lilly traced my chest with her fingers.

"Now, you stop distracting me." I grinned.

"I'm going with you."

I didn't say anything. I let her continue touching me, because fact was, I loved it. I held her close, listening to the soft sounds of her breathing once she finally fell asleep. I had no intention of letting her go with me. When she woke up tomorrow morning. I'd be gone and my father would answer for what he had done.

Chapter Thirty-four: Lilly

1937

It was slightly dark, with the morning sun not yet fully risen. I rolled over and found Christopher still lying in bed. His arm was draped across his face, masking his eyes and fully exposing his chest.

I reached for him, tracing my fingers across every inch of his body. He lifted his arm, an opening allowing his gaze to greet me.

"Good Morning," I said, trailing my fingers down further. Everything with Christopher just fell into place. I never would have imagined myself doing any of this with another man or before marriage. Here, in his arms felt right.

"Well, good morning to you too."

I stopped at the sheet, removing it slowly. It was like unwrapping a present. I loved surprises and what was underneath this sheet was slowly becoming one of my favorites. I licked my lips in anticipation then took the base of him in my hand while working the rest of him with my mouth. I changed my speed based on the sounds that came from him. He grasped my hair, a feeling of pain and pleasure radiating throughout my body.

This was something that I could get used to. Waking up next to Christopher. Pleasuring him in every way possible.

"Don't stop, Lilly, I'm almost there."

Christopher released his grasp on my hair to let me up, but I didn't. I continued pleasuring him. A warm sensation filled my mouth, and I swallowed all his cum, licking my lips to be sure I didn't miss a single drop of him.

"Lilly, I think I'm in love with you." He laughed and brought me in for a kiss.

I knew he was joking. The laugh that accompanied the words told me that, but something in me stirred. I wanted his words to be true.

"I need to take a shower and get ready to see your father."

Christopher stiffened against me. I knew this was a tough subject for him—what his father had done—but I was determined to be there to confront Fredrick. To uncover the truth behind what had happened to my mother and father.

"Okay." Christopher swung his legs over the bed then stood.

He was a sight, a wonderful sight that I never wanted to stop seeing.

"I'm going to run you a bath. So you can relax." He looked back at me as he put on his underwear. "I bet you're sore." A devilish grin curled on his lips.

"A little bit. But I don't mind." I didn't mind. At all. Everything ached, but it was dull in comparison to the pleasure that had overcome me. The pleasure of his hands touching my body, his lips against mine, the fullness I felt each time he'd thrust himself into me. My head fell into the pillow as the need for Christopher to be inside me heightened.

"I'll be back. Don't go anywhere." He bent over and placed a kiss to my forehead.

I waited, my mind drifting between the night I had shared with Christopher and what I was bound to uncover today. I was ready for the truth.

The door creaked open from the bathroom and Christopher walked in. He gathered me in his arms. I didn't fight him. There was something about his movements, the look in his eyes that comforted me and told me he needed to hold me close. He carried me into the bathroom, gently placing me down in the bathtub filled with bubbles. It was warm, and I winced when the water hit me.

"See, you are in pain." He pecked a kiss to my cheek. "Let me wash you." He reached for the washcloth and washed and lathered me up. The sex with Christopher had been great. But this, it was sensual, a simple act that made me want him even more.

"I'm going to let you relax."

The bathroom door latched behind him as he left me in the bath. It felt good against my sore muscles, releasing the tension that had built there. I allowed myself to drift off. I didn't know how much time had passed, but when I took my hands out of the water, they had turned wrinkled and soft. I got out of the water, wrapping a towel around my body then padded into the bedroom.

The sun had fully come up and was bright and comforting. Although I knew what I was going to face today, the day held promise. Promise that maybe everything wasn't going to turn out so bad.

After dressing, I went down to the kitchen to find Virginia and Jeremiah sitting at the table.

"Where's Christopher?" I said as I opened the refrigerator and took out the water pitcher, pouring myself a glass.

"He left," Jeremiah mumbled through his bite of food.

"He what?" I nearly dropped my water glass. "Where?" I couldn't believe he left. I talked myself down from the anger, thinking that maybe he was called into work.

Jeremiah shrugged, and Virginia avoided my stare. She knew something, much more than she was divulging.

"Doesn't it matter to you that he ran off this morning after leaving all day yesterday. After finding out what your father did?" I moved closer to Jeremiah.

He stopped eating and glared at me. "He's a grown man.

He can handle himself."

I understood that sentiment. I really did. But after last night and Christopher telling me that his father would pay, I couldn't help but wonder how far he was willing to go.

"Against your father?" Virginia said. The sound of her chair scuffing against the kitchen floor filled the silence that had fallen. The silence was all I needed to know.

"Exactly. You know it isn't a good idea to let him go there alone." I sighed. "You and I both know that's where he is right now."

Virginia came back into the room.

"Scarlett's on her way."

Jeremiah and I both turned and stared at her.

"She has a car. We need to get there and fast."

"There's no we." Jeremiah said. "I'll go and handle this."

I grunted. "Over my dead body."

"That's exactly what's going to happen if you come along. This is something that Christopher and I need to handle alone with our father!" Jeremiah was yelling, leaning across the table. A vein on the side of head was protruding.

I got it. This man was their father. But it was my mother who was raped. My parents who were murdered.

"No." I went and wrapped my arms around Jeremiah. His shoulders tensed but I squeezed tighter and he loosened up slightly. "Fredrick is your and Christopher's father. I understand that." I let him go and stared at him. "But it was our mother who was raped and murdered."

He ground his teeth.

"It was my father who was murdered as well. So, let me go. Let me get the answers that I need as badly as you and Christopher."

Jeremiah studied me thoughtfully. "Okay." He sighed. "You're a pain in my ass, you know that?"

I smiled. "Well, I'm your little sister. It's my job."

He pulled me in for a hug and kissed my cheek.

"Look at me!" Virginia dabbed her eyes with her napkin. "I always thought about the day I'd see my daughter again. I know now that won't happen, but this," she said as she motioned between us. "This is like heaven. My two grandbabies together."

I gave her a quick hug.

"Please be safe. You are all I've got left," she said to us.

I looked at Virginia and my brother and realized there was a lot more at stake now than before. I had come here, just myself, with nothing to lose. Now, I'd gained a family

A loud horn outside broke into our conversation and Jeremiah and I both headed out to Scarlett's car.

"Where to?" she asked gripping the steering wheel. She was ready, wearing a pair of simple slacks and top with a pair of flats. It was subtle compared to her normal flashy outfits.

"My father's," Jeremiah said, settling into the back seat.

She sped off, heading to what I assumed was Fredrick's house. For a moment, I was thankful for a friend like her.

Then the concern crept in.

I remembered yesterday, me telling her that Jeremiah was my brother. But I'd never told her Fredrick was his father. My heart beat loudly in my chest. Scarlett turned and smiled at me.

I glanced toward the back of the car. Jeremiah sat staring out the window, oblivious to anything out of the ordinary. I had to figure out how to warn him about what Scarlett knew that she shouldn't. I thought I had a friend in Scarlett, but maybe what I had was another enemy.

Chapter Thirty-Five: Christopher

1937

"Dad?" I walked through the house, calling my father's name. I had to come and talk to him, alone. I knew Jeremiah and Lilly deserved answers, but I wanted to hear him say it first. Hear him say all the things he had done to Iris.

All those years of him teaching me and Tucker his ideology. Shoving down our throats that blacks had no place in our town, in any town. I'd been able to draw my own conclusions, but not Tucker. No, that hate had had an impact on him, and he mirrored my father in almost everything he did.

I walked into my father's office. He was staring out the window. He didn't greet me. I looked at my father—really looked at him for the first time in a long time. His hair was white. Wrinkles lined the corners of his eyes. He was aging. Aging more than I had realized.

"Son have a seat. I know why you're here." He turned to face me—his eyes were swollen by tears. They were red rimmed and glistening and it caught me off guard. I'd never seen my father like this. I'd never seen him anything but completely poised. I almost felt sorry for him.

Almost.

I remembered the rape, a brother he had treated poorly because he was of mixed race. And my remorse was quickly replaced with the anger I was accustomed to.

"Why'd you do it?" I didn't have to explain. He knew what I was referring to.

He sighed, putting his face in his hands. "Nothing is ever as it looks Christopher . . ."

"I don't care. Tell me the truth. I deserve at least that. Your son, Jeremiah, deserves at least that."

"I loved Iris. More than I ever loved your mother."

I sat back and listened, taking each word he said and committing them to my memory, because after my father told me the truth, things would be different.

I wouldn't let Lilly or Jeremiah near him. I hadn't protected Jeremiah when we were children, but I could do it now. And Lilly would never get to meet my father. He didn't deserve to know her. To realize how smart and beautiful she was. How she made me want to be a better man, question everything I had ever learned, and everything I ever believed.

"Iris came into Charles' and my life at a time when Charles and I were always together." He smiled, and I wondered if he was thinking about his past. "God, she was beautiful. Her dark skin, eyes that lit up her face. She was unlike anything I'd ever seen. But she was forbidden. Charles won her over. He didn't care what other people thought. He loved her and that was enough. Love wasn't enough for me. Mixing races was wrong. It is wrong." He moved towards the desk and slammed his fists against it.

"That's where you're wrong, Dad. Love is love. It doesn't matter about skin color, religion, any of that garbage that we've been fed. It's bullshit."

He beamed. "You sound like Charles. It's true then?" He sat down. "Lilly?"

I nodded.

"Just like her mother, stealing hearts."

Lilly was a heart-stealer. I'd give my father that. She had walked into my life and from that moment, there was no one else for me. Just her. We were meant to be. So yes, I guess I was like Charles. I would do anything for her. Which was why I was here confronting my father. To get answers. To uncover the truth.

"I'm not here to bond. Why did you rape Iris and force her to leave Jeremiah behind? That's evil. Worse than anything I ever imagined you could do."

"I was angry that Charles was able to push aside everything we had ever been taught and raised to believe, to follow his heart. I envied him and how he was always able to go with what he believed in. He didn't struggle. There was fear, sure, but that fear was secondary to doing what was right." He shook his head. "I was . . ." He hung his head in shame. "I am weak. It's easier to follow what everyone else is doing than to question it."

"You raped Iris. That's beyond following what everyone else was doing. That's a crime."

"I was angry, Son. I don't think you understand what anger will do to a person. I was brave and I told Iris I loved her, but she just told me her heart belonged to Charles. I couldn't see beyond my own pain, so I did what I did." He stood straighter. "I'm not proud of any of it. I have a lot of regrets. A lot of things that I should have done differently."

"And Jeremiah? Why did you treat him so poorly?" I leaned forward. "You used to beat him for no reason. For being happy and living his life. That's no father."

"He was a reminder of Iris. Every day I looked at him, he was a reminder of what I did to her. I was ashamed." Tears rimmed my father's eyes. "I am ashamed."

"Your tears won't bring Iris and Charles back from you murdering them—whipping her, shooting him."

A tear fell down his face as he looked at me. "Son, I admit I raped Iris all those years ago, but I didn't kill her or Charles. I loved her. Even till her dying day I loved that woman."

"Fuck!" I said, pacing the floor. I was hell bent on my father being the murderer that I hadn't thought of anyone else. Who would have such a vendetta and an issue with Charles and Iris that they would go as far as to kill them?

"Tucker," my father whispered.

My brother.

"Why? He didn't know about you and Iris until I did."

My father shook his head. "He found out a while ago. After an um, meeting with Scarlett. She was helping me pack up some old photos. There was another photo of me and Iris and Jeremiah as an infant. He asked, and I couldn't deny it."

Scarlett.

I hadn't thought about her since our encounter in my office when I turned her down. She knew all along about my father and Iris. What is she willing to do with that information?

"Why keep that picture?"

He shrugged. "It was all I had of her other than Jeremiah. I hadn't been a father to him, so it wasn't like I could talk to him about her." He sat in the chair and looked even more distant—lost in a memory of a woman he'd loved but who hadn't loved him.

"I have to bring Tucker in for this. Someone has to pay for what happened to Iris and Charles."

My father stood, the chair scraping the floor. "I'm coming with you. He won't go quietly."

What my father had done was horrible, raping a woman against her will, bringing a son into this world and treating him like a servant. He'd answer for what he'd done. But for now, this wasn't about him or me.

"Alright. Let's go."

My own brother would be on the receiving end of the justice I so badly wanted to serve.

Chapter Thirty-six: Lilly

1937

"Where are we going?" I pulled tighter on my seatbelt as we passed by the turn that should have been for the Mayor's house. I was still new around here, but the town was small, it was hard to not know where you were going.

"To where it all happened." Scarlett stared forward.

"What?" The alarm in his voice made the hairs on my arms stand on end. Then I felt it, the cool metal of a gun against my forehead.

"Stay back, Jeremiah, or I'll shoot her. Your precious sister." Scarlett snickered as she held the wheel with one hand and pointed the gun against my temple with the other.

I had been naïve. Too blinded by my desire to have a friend to see Scarlett was playing me by pretending to care about me and what was happening.

"Why, Scarlett?"

She turned down a long gravel road, and the gun scraped against my head with each bump. "He's going to marry me." Her bright smile jarred me. Jeremiah cursed under his breath.

"Who? Christopher?"

Keep her talking. The more she talks the better.

"No!" She screamed, slamming on her brakes. "You ruined us getting married." She waved the gun in my face. "Get out. Both of you." She glanced back at Jeremiah as we got out of the car.

"Either of you try anything, and I'll shoot."

Jeremiah took my hand in his, and we walked through the woods.

"Tucker." Jeremiah shook his head in disbelief as we rounded the corner. Standing there was Tucker, his arms crossed over his chest.

"Brother," he said sarcastically.

"Baby," Scarlett went to move towards Tucker.

"Stay over there! Keep the gun on them. Jeremiah can't be left unguarded."

Scarlett scuffled back as reality settled in for me. This had all been about Tucker. She had settled for the only brother who would give her the time of day. I felt a twinge of sadness when I looked at Scarlett. She craved getting married — to have a man with a decent standing in society — so much that she was willing to be an accomplice to a crime.

"Tie him to the tree." Tucker threw Scarlett some rope and she caught it with one hand. He moved quickly towards me, right as Jeremiah lunged out at him. They wrestled on the ground, rolling over and over, trading punches. Scarlett was startled by their fighting and leaped out of the way. As Jeremiah fought with Tucker, I took my opportunity to try to disarm Scarlett.

I elbowed her in the stomach, and she bent forward, grasping her stomach and dropping the gun. As I went to reach for it, Tucker snatched the gun up then pointed it at me. I searched frantically for Jeremiah, who lay on the ground. He wasn't moving. My brother. A brother I had just gotten, would probably die in these woods. *I* would probably die in these woods. My fate would be that of my parents. At least I'd die knowing what the love of a man felt like. I had made love for the first time and knew what it was like to be embraced by those I loved.

"Go to the tree."

I walked over to the tree, then sat in front of it. Scarlett tied my arms behind me. I stared at Tucker—I wasn't scared. There was a cowardice about a man who had to wield a gun and prey on people all because of the color of their skin. If this was how my life was going to end, I welcomed it. But I wouldn't go down without a fight.

"You're so much like your momma." He snickered as he walked away.

"You're a coward. Hiding behind your gun."

He spun around and looked at me.

"Tying me up and what? Shooting me? For what reason?" I asked.

I felt a sting across my face. Scarlett loomed over me, shaking out the hand she'd used to smack me.

"Don't talk to him like that!" She kicked me in the stomach.

I breathed through the pain.

"You waltz into the police department demanding help and bat those pretty little eyes, and Christopher falls at your feet. It's wrong! Wrong!" Scarlett screamed.

Tucker launched himself at Scarlett and gripped her by her hair, throwing her against a nearby tree. A loud crack filled the air, then she crumbled to the ground.

"You killed her," I said stunned. I looked at her crumpled body, contorted. I had thought Scarlett was my friend. Her betrayal came as a surprise, but no one deserved to be murdered. Especially not like this. "You threw her like she was—"

"Nothing?" he interrupted me. "She was nothing. Scarlett wanted to get married and have a bunch of kids. I promised her those things and she agreed to win you over and gain information." Tucker moved over to a bag that was on the ground then pulled out a whip.

I shuddered. This was what my mother had shielded me from, a life that she'd lived decades ago. Now I was waiting to live it. I rested my head against the tree.

Momma, please make me strong.

"Open your eyes, Lilly. I want you to see what I'm about to do to you."

The silky, cold leather of the whip caressed my cheek. I was trying to be brave, pushing aside my thoughts and emotions, but a tear fell, and Tucker laughed.

He positioned the front of me to the tree, my hands now tied in front. He ripped the dress from my body, my underwear, my cami. I was naked, exposed in flesh to a man too blinded by the hate and pain that his father had taught him. Exposed in body, but not in mind.

I went back to my stolen moments with Christopher. To the days we had shared together, the nights in which he showed me with his hands, his mouth how much I meant to him. I let my mind stay with Christopher as the whip slashed against my back over and over again. I thought I had protected myself. Shielded my mind from the pain. I saw Christopher's face, flitting in and out and I cried through the pain.

"Don't leave me." I begged. "Please."

A booming laugh filled the air and one last time the whip cracked against my back. I searched for solace in thoughts of Christopher, but he was gone. Everything was gone and it was just me, left in darkness.

Chapter Thirty-Seven: Christopher

1937

"Jesus fucking Christ!" I ran fast and hard, my father trying to keep up behind me. I heard it, the crack of the whip and her voice. Her voice begging and pleading.

The scene in front me made me reel in shock, vomit surfaced in my throat, and everything began to spin. I took a deep breath and tried to process everything that was hitting me at once.

Lilly was tied to the same tree her mother had died against, her back covered in open wounds, seeping with blood. Her head bobbed to the side. Jeremiah was lying on the ground, a large wound on the side of his head, blood pooling next to him. Scarlett was laying on the ground, her back in an odd position.

And then, there was my brother, the little brother I had walked with to school every day, the little brother who I'd played tag with, standing behind the woman I loved, holding a whip dripping with blood.

"Don't." My father grabbed my arm as I reached for my gun. "You'll never be able to live with yourself. Let me talk to him."

I didn't want to talk. I didn't want to hear what he had to say. There was something about seeing the woman who had suddenly become my everything exposed and beaten that made me lose all sense of rationality. I wanted him dead.

"Tucker?" Fredrick moved slowly towards Tucker.

Tucker turned around and dropped the whip at his side. "Dad? What are you doing here?" His eyes were big and round as he stared back at me. For a moment, he was a young boy again, eagerly wanting his father's approval. Maybe my dad was right, he needed to be talked to.

"I'm here to take you home."

Tucker tilted his head to the side as he studied our father and me for a minute.

"It's over, Tucker. You made your point," I added.

"I can't come home now. Not after what I've done." He shook his head, the determination returning across his face.

"What did you do, Tucker?" I wanted him to say it. To put it all into words so I could without a doubt shove him into a cell for the rest of his life.

"I killed Iris and Charles." He paused, glancing back at Jeremiah, Lilly, and Scarlett. "And them too."

"No," I said calmly.

She wasn't dead. She couldn't be.

"Sorry, brother." He laughed. "I couldn't let you fall for Lilly like Dad did for Iris. And having Jeremiah for a brother? That wouldn't be good for our family line. We're Weatherby's."

I ripped my gun out and rushed towards him to put the pistol against his forehead.

"Do it!" he cried, egging me on like we were playing a game, like we were still children. "Kill your full, purebred brother over a fucking half-bred, a whore, and a woman who has no place here." He grabbed the gun and pushed it harder against his head. "Fucking do it!"

Lilly groaned, and I dropped the gun and ran to be near her. Tucker didn't deserve to be killed. He didn't deserve to escape the guilt of having to live with what he had done. Lilly was right. Violence was not the answer.

"Lilly?"

She groaned again, and I slowly untied her, bringing her away from the tree. I was careful not to touch her wounds. The last thing I wanted to do was cause her any more pain.

I brushed her matted hair from her face and laid her on her stomach. I took off my jacket then covered her body. I couldn't bring myself to look at her back. Blood was everywhere and there was no doubt she'd be scarred for the rest of her life. But she was alive. God was I grateful she was alive.

"I love you, Lilly," I whispered into her ear.

The click of a gun sharpened my focus. I'd made a choice just now. A choice that Lilly mattered more to me than revenge. If death was my sentence for not sticking up sooner for what was right, then so be it. At least I knew the woman I loved was alive.

A gun shot rang out, but the pain never came. I reached around and touched the back of my head expecting to feel blood but there was nothing. I opened my eyes, turned to see my father holding a smoking gun. Tucker lay on the ground.

"He was going to kill you." My father's hands were shaking violently. I hurried towards my father then took the gun from his hands.

"It's okay, Dad."

He fell to his knees and wept. Sobs quaked through his body. I left him there, to cry for a woman he'd loved. A woman he raped, a son he killed, and a son who'd died all because of his father's ignorance and hate.

I carried the woman I loved, broken and bloody, to the car. I went back for my brother. I took them both home — to Virginia. Where she could heal Lilly and she could move forward from everything that had happened. Where she could be with the family she had left and surrounded by people who loved her.

Chapter Thirty-eight: Lilly

1937

Nothing was ever as it seemed. I had been able to live a decent childhood. Virtually unscathed by the past that had haunted my mother and father. Until now.

My eyes fluttered open, my back aching like a thousand daggers were shooting through it. I couldn't move my arms. Everything hurt.

"Lilly?" Christopher's face came into focus as I fully opened my eyes and saw him sitting in the chair. It all came back to me, the lashes, Scarlett and Tucker both wanting Jeremiah and I dead.

"It's okay, You're safe now." Christopher grabbed my hand.

"It hurts . . ." Was all I managed to get out.

"I'll change your dressings."

I bit back the screams as Christopher slowly cut the bandages from my back. Some stuck, resulting in him having to use a little force to remove them. Then my pain didn't matter anymore as I remembered Jeremiah laying on the ground unconscious.

"Jeremiah?" I breathed out.

"He's alive. Thank God. He's unresponsive but breathing. I've got the doctor here around the clock, Lilly. I won't let anything happen to either of you."

The pain had become too much to bear. My mind couldn't rationalize all my emotions. Jeremiah hanging on to his life, the excruciating pain that spread throughout my body. It was too much. My mind shielded me from the pain, taking me away from it all.

I was greeted by parents. Both smiling, hand in hand as they stood out by a lake just like they used to when they snuck away to be together. They looked young, peaceful, and un-plagued by the hate that had taken them away from me too soon.

"Mom, Dad," I called out to them.

They smiled, and as I placed my hands in theirs, warmth envel-oped my body, the pain gone.

"Am I dying?"

My mother reached out and caressed my cheek. "No child. Your time on this earth isn't over. You'll live a full, joyful life."

I nodded as the tears streamed down my face. I didn't want to die. My body was broken, sure, but I had so much left to do. So much that I wanted to accomplish.

"Love him, Lilly. Love him like I loved your mother. With una-bridged passion. No fear. No remorse." My father leaned over and kissed my mother on the forehead.

They didn't have to say his name. I knew who they were talking about. Christopher.

"And take care of my boy. I never wanted to leave Jeremiah."

"Fredrick loved you, Mom. In his own messed up way. He saved me. He saved Christopher and Jeremiah."

"I know, child. People do crazy things. I was angry that he took me against my will. I struggled for a long time with what happened. But your father's love, his faith in kindness, and a world that could change helped me to move on. And you, sweet child. Having you brought me such joy."

The sun that was shining on the lake started to go down, and I knew our time was coming to an end.

"I don't want you to leave. I miss you both so much." I held my-self, trying to keep the sobs that threatened to break free at bay.

"We're always with you, Lilly. We're the sun in the sky. The color in the world. Your father and I will always be with you."

I knew they'd stay true to their word and forever be by my side and that was enough for me to let them go.

Chapter Thirty-nine: Christopher

1967

We had been through so much. Lilly took months to heal from the wounds that Tucker had inflicted on her. Jeremiah was in a coma for two weeks before waking up and wanting to kill Tucker. He was pleased when he heard our father had done it for him.

Our father was long gone, never to be seen again after the day he took his own son's life. I was sure the regret was too much for him and the fate he faced here too great to stay. I was grateful for him protecting me that day.

"Governor?" One of my assistants rushed to me on the patio and handed me a paper. I'd been Governor for a while now and had managed to change the areas that once had been so corrupt and plagued by hate. It wasn't easy, and some days I thought that after over thirty years, things would never change but today, today was different.

"Yes?" I asked taking the paper from him.

"This is it. Loving vs. Virginia, they won".

I gripped the paper hard, my mouth going dry. This was it.

"Thank you"

He nodded and walked away.

I sat back in the chair. I had been waiting for this. Decades for our government to get their act together and allow interracial marriage to be legal.

And I was their strongest supporter. I gathered the paper and headed back into the house.

Lilly was laying on our bed, her eyes closed. She looked peaceful, a small contented smile curving her beautiful lips. Time had been kind to us. Allowing us to live out our lives with our daughter and son and teaching them love and acceptance. But the one thing that never changed was that Lilly and I had never been able to marry.

Today, that would change.

"Lilly?"

Her eyes flitted open.

"Hello." She patted the bed next to her. Everything Lilly did was done out of love. She was perfection.

"Hello." I brushed a chaste kiss to her lips. "Have I ever told you how much I love you?"

She laughed. "Every day, Christopher. Every day for many, many years." She closed her eyes again.

"Lilly . . ."

She opened her eyes and sat up. "What's wrong?"

"Nothing's wrong. I just wanted to ask you something."

She stared at me.

"Today marks an important day for us. Do you remember all those years ago, you walked into the police station and demanded I investigate your parents' murder?"

She nodded. "I remember." She cupped my cheek with her hand.

"Today, North Carolina struck down all state laws banning interracial marriage."

Tears fell down Lilly's cheeks.

She took the paper from my hand and read it. Every single word. It was the lawyer in her.

Lilly had opened a small office and took cases pertaining to racial injustices, equality, anything along those lines. She was living her dream. That was all I had ever wanted for her.

"I can't believe it." She laughed through her tears.

"Marry me, Lilly? Right here, where it all started for your

parents. Marry me so our children will know the love that their parents share is real."

She placed the papers on the bed. "I don't need a silly piece of paper to know that what we have is real, Christopher."

I braced myself for another denial.

"But I always wanted to be Mrs. Weatherby. From the moment I saw you in your police uniform, to giving birth to your children, nothing would make me happier than marrying you."

I placed my lips gently down hers, took her in my arms, and we laid back together on the bed. I glanced over at her. Her eyes were closed, her breathing making her chest to move up and down. Her hair was now graying, and faint wrinkles had formed around the corner of her eyes. Those were my favorite because they reminded me of all the times we laughed together. All the joy that our love and life had brought to us. I put my hand in hers, and we stayed that way basking in how wonderful our life turned out.

I thought about what a lucky man I was. There was nothing more I wanted in my life. I had a beautiful family and had watched our children grow into incredible adults.

Now I was making a difference in the world, standing up for what I believed in, and being a voice for equality. All of this because of Lillian Pearl Porter, who'd walked into my life demanding justice and had made me see things differently.

She'd made me see things for what they were, not black and white, but multiple colors that merged into each other and made a beautiful picture. A picture similar to the one I was a part of now. A picture that held the promise of change, and the promise of a world fueled by equality, hope and love. It was the promise of a life worth living.

YOU MAY ALSO ENJOY THE FOLLOWING FROM EXTASY BOOKS INC:

Meant to Be
Gen Ryan

Excerpt

With a coffee in one hand and my cell phone in the other, I navigated through the busy streets of downtown Boston. It was my first week here, and I was solo. No boyfriend. No friends. Just me in the big city. Starting fresh.

The crisp air gave way to cooler weather and Halloween was just around the corner. I was a sucker for candy and cute little ones in costumes. A few storefronts were decorated for Halloween, pumpkins and skeletons lining their windows and stairs. I loved fall in New England.

Some days I was lonely. But that was okay. I had a brand-new job at the prestigious literary company, Ink and Pen. I was riding high, not letting anything from my past interfere with my accomplishments.

"What the hell!" I raised my head as my coffee flew from my hands and spilt all over my nicely pressed white shirt. Of course, the cup of hot, delicious goodness hit the ground, and it splattered all over my beige heels.

I danced in place as the heat of the coffee seeped into my

toes and against my chest.

"I'm so sorry. Seems we both were distracted." A man well over six feet tall stood in front of me. His jeans and plain shirt were unscathed from the coffee disaster that had just happened. Which made sense, considering he looked like he'd been plunked right from the heavens. He was a cross between a Greek god and an Abercrombie model. Naturally, the universe would be kind to him.

"It's fine." I sighed and pulled my shirt away from my skin. Why I'd decided to be cute and wear a patterned bra was beyond me.

"Here." The man took off his shirt, revealing a black tank top underneath. And tattoos. Lots and lots of tattoos.

I found it hard not to gawp—okay, well, stare—at the ink that peppered his mocha skin. There were words, a few things that resembled faces, and things I couldn't decipher. I smiled at a small jack-o'-lantern woven between some words about seizing the day. I love Halloween. I usually wasn't a fan of tattoos, but this perfect stranger was a piece of art. Someone worthy of being gawked at. Which I was doing.

Focus.

"No! Please. It's fine. I'll just grab another shirt." My phoned buzzed, reminding me I had to be at Ink and Pen in a half hour to fill out new hire paperwork.

"I have lots at my office. Take it. Don't want people ogling your flower-patterned bra, do you?" He winked and held out his shirt.

Who was I to deny this perfect gentleman his chivalrous act? Plus, I liked admiring his arms. I shrugged.

"Thank you." I tugged the shirt over my body. It was way too big, but it did the trick. I caught a whiff of his cologne and resisted the urge to bring it to my nose and sniff it. That would officially make me creepy.

"Better tell your boyfriend what happened when you go home in another man's shirt," the stranger added.

"No boyfriend." I laughed as I caught a glimpse of my

reflection in the store window. I resembled a child wearing an oversized sleep shirt. All I needed was pigtails, and it'd complete the ensemble.

"Well, in that case, I'm Chase." We shook hands. "Can I replace that coffee? There's a shop around the corner. And our current attire would fit right in."

We both snorted at the craziness of our appearances.

"I'd love to, but I have a meeting in a half hour. Rain check?" Riffling through my purse, I took out a wet wipe and tried my best to salvage my shoes. Thank God it was just paperwork and not my official first day. I was working closely with the head of the company and wanted to make a good first impression. Having coffee-stained shoes and wearing the shirt of a man I'd just met wasn't what I had in mind.

"How about dinner, tonight?"

"Oh, um . . ." My phone buzzed again. Dammit. I was barely going to make it.

"Here, put in your number." Chase handed me his cell, and I entered it. "Perfect. I'll give you a call, and we can set something up. Willow. That's a beautiful name for a beautiful girl."

"Flattery will get you everywhere, Chase. But I have to go. Pleasure to run into you. And thanks for your shirt."

"Anytime you need a shirt. Some pants. I'm your guy." He pointed his thumbs at himself.

Cheesy. But adorable. "Noted! Take care!" I smiled and waved as I walked away.

When I knew I was out of his sight, I brought his shirt closer to my face and took in a deep breath.

This fumbled encounter might turn into something. Or not. But either way, Boston was seeming to be exactly what I needed.

ABOUT THE AUTHOR

Gen Ryan is an international best-selling author and forensic psychologist who spends her days molding the next generation of forensic psychologists. Each semester she starts with profiling, moves to interrogation, and ends on a high note with her absolute favorite, serial killers.

Her nights are spent crafting stories that will tear a reader's heart out and twist their minds at the same time. She brings a unique twist to romance, a twist always rooted somewhere deep inside the character's psyche that will keep readers on the edge of their seats.